THE EX-FILES

'But you'll help me get Nicole back?'

He shook his head. 'This is definitely not a dating
service . . . In fact, really it's exactly the opposite.
Our job is to help you put a relationship behind
you . . . which, believe me, can be one of the
hardest things in the world . . . especially when
you're a teenager, going through it for the very first
time. Yet not one single person seems to understand
or be able to help. You're totally alone.'

'Until now,' I interrupted, 'with the Ex-Files riding
to your rescue.' My tone was a shade mocking but
actually I was becoming more and more intrigued
by this whole set-up.

Pete Johnson has been a film extra, a film critic for Radio 1, an English teacher and a journalist. However, his dream was always to be a writer. At the age of ten, he wrote a fan letter to Dodie Smith, author of *The Hundred and One Dalmatians*, and they wrote to each other for many years. Dodie Smith was the first person to encourage him to be a writer.

He has written many books for children, as well as plays for the theatre and Radio 4, and is a popular visitor to schools and libraries.

petejohnsonauthor.com

Some other books by Pete Johnson

THE COOL BOFFIN
THE EX-FILES
FAKING IT
THE HERO GAME
I'D RATHER BE FAMOUS
TEN HOURS TO LIVE

For younger readers

PIRATE BROTHER

THE EX-FILES

PETE JOHNSON

PUFFIN

PUFFIN BOOKS

Published by the Penguin Group
Penguin Books Ltd, 80 Strand, London WC2R 0RL, England
Penguin Group (USA) Inc., 375 Hudson Street, New York, New York 10014, USA
Penguin Group (Canada), 90 Eglinton Avenue East, Suite 700, Toronto, Ontario, Canada M4P 2Y3
(a division of Pearson Penguin Canada Inc.)
Penguin Ireland, 25 St Stephen's Green, Dublin 2, Ireland (a division of Penguin Books Ltd)
Penguin Group (Australia), 250 Camberwell Road, Camberwell, Victoria 3124, Australia
(a division of Pearson Australia Group Pty Ltd)
Penguin Books India Pvt Ltd, 11 Community Centre, Panchsheel Park, New Delhi – 110 017, India
Penguin Group (NZ), cnr Airborne and Rosedale Roads, Albany, Auckland 1310, New Zealand
(a division of Pearson New Zealand Ltd)
Penguin Books (South Africa) (Pty) Ltd, 24 Sturdee Avenue, Rosebank, Johannesburg 2196, South Africa

Penguin Books Ltd, Registered Offices: 80 Strand, London WC2R 0RL, England

penguin.com

First published 2006
1

Copyright © Pete Johnson, 2006
All rights reserved

The moral right of the author has been asserted

Set in 11.5/15.5 pt Goudy
Typeset by Palimpsest Book Production Limited, Polmont, Stirlingshire
Made and printed in England by Clays Ltd, St Ives plc

British Library Cataloguing in Publication Data
A CIP catalogue record for this book is available from the British Library

ISBN-13: 978-0-141-31983-4
ISBN-10: 0-141-31983-6

This book is dedicated to the great unsung heroes – and heroines – of the Children's Book World: the librarians

With grateful thanks and admiration

Contents

PART ONE

Two Stories

BELLA'S STORY

Chapter 1

THURSDAY 23 JUNE

Today I cut up my best friend's favourite dress.

I can't even say I did it in a moment of crazed anguish. It was totally premeditated. I'd spent ages searching for the right pair of scissors – I wanted the especially sharp ones.

I knew Andrea was away visiting her dad this afternoon, so here was my chance to get inside her bedroom. And it was dead easy. I told her mum I thought I'd lost a special earring there. My only worry was that she might stay and look for it with me (she's one of those very eager-to-please mums). But luckily the phone rang, leaving me to carry out my act of vengeance in peace.

I located the dress at once. Well, it was impossible to miss. The one Andrea had been all day choosing. The one she planned to wear to her birthday party on Saturday.

Hot, angry tears shot down my face as I cut it up.

Andrea and I have been best friends ever since I moved here last October. She's so self-confident and lively and always right in the centre of things – exactly how I would like to be. You might even say I wasn't only her friend; I was her fan as well.

Our friendship really took off the day she had her belly button pierced. She was so nervous she wanted someone to go with her – and I volunteered. I remember telling her to take lots of deep breaths and she quipped, 'I'm not having a baby, you know.'

Andrea got into big trouble when her mum discovered what she'd done, but she and I became so close after that. Later she told me very personal stuff about her family that I'd never reveal to another person. We completely trusted each other. That's why I never, ever thought she'd betray me – and in the very worst way possible.

I scattered the dress's remains all over the wardrobe. I wasn't just burying a dress; I was burying a friendship as well.

Suddenly I heard one of the stairs creak. The sound shot through me like a jolt of electricity. I leaped away from the wardrobe as if it had bitten me. I'd just managed to fling the scissors under the bed when a voice asked, 'Any luck?'

Andrea's mum was smiling sympathetically at me – but was there a glimmer of suspicion in her eyes too?

I said, with an apologetic grin, 'Actually, I think I must have left the earring somewhere else.'

'Oh, I see,' she said, but was still looking at me a trifle oddly. I thought suddenly, *You know what Andrea's done to me, don't you? You know everything.*

She said, 'Never mind, dear, I'm sure it'll turn up . . .

and I expect you're very glad to have broken up for the summer holidays, aren't you?'

'Oh yes,' I started to reply. Then, from out of the corner of my eye, I noticed the wardrobe door was moving. It was as if invisible strings were slowly pulling it open again.

I sprang forward. But Andrea's mum was right beside me. 'I'm afraid that door has to be pushed very hard . . . Oh!' she cried out suddenly. She crouched down. 'Oh no,' she yelped again, then turned to me, her whole face wobbling with shock.

I didn't stay to chat. In fact, I hurtled down the stairs and out of the house at a speed which would have amazed my PE teacher.

At home I gloated for a bit. When Andrea returns, what a shock she'll get. She'll realize at once that I know everything.

But my feeling of triumph didn't last very long. And afterwards I just felt more confused and lost than ever.

I still can't make any sense of what's happened. Ever since I got back from holiday on Monday it's as if I've plunged into some bizarre new life, where the most awful and totally weird things just keep happening.

And now I've started cutting up dresses – well, one dress. I can honestly say that is something I would never have imagined myself doing. It seems so petty and downright nasty.

'But Andrea deserved it.' That phrase keeps jumping into my head. I wondered, suddenly, if she'll tell Luc what I've done. Yes, she's bound to do that; she'll be so indignant and upset, milking it for all the sympathy she can get. 'You won't believe what Bella's done!' she'll cry. Only Luc will reply – and I can practically hear him – 'But that isn't like Bella at all.' There'll be a little worried frown on his face, too.

Then he'll ring me, just to check I'm all right.

And here's the really awful thing: despite everything he's done, I'm looking forward to Luc's call already. In fact, I'm writing this with my mobile right beside me, waiting.

WAITING.

Chapter 2

FRIDAY 24 JUNE
11.30 a.m.

I'm lying in bed with the curtains drawn (told Dad I had a bad migraine), listening to music. I've selected all my favourites and I can't hear any of them. All I can hear is the phone not ringing. That's so deafening it drowns out everything else.

Why hasn't Luc rung just to check I'm all right? I did go out with him for seven months.

Then there's Andrea. Not that I want to talk to her. Ever. But I'd rather have her screeching down the phone about my twisted act of revenge than this thick, heavy silence.

1.45 p.m.

I've just done something very stupid: I told Dad about Luc and me breaking up. I hadn't before because, well, my dad's great in so many ways, but he likes good news, happy stuff . . . something like this is a bit outside his field of expertise. But I'd just got through one of those mornings that seems to last forever, and Dad had come home specially at lunchtime because he was worried about me.

This touched me so much I revealed everything (well, except for the bit about me vandalizing Andrea's dress). And Dad sat there, looking pained and embarrassed at the same time. And when I'd finished he gave me a little hug which was nice and some advice which was completely useless.

'What you've got to do now, Bella,' he said, 'is throw this boy, Luc, back in the pond and find someone much better . . . which I promise you, you will.'

'Thanks a lot, Dad,' I said wearily, and then added, 'You'd better go back to work now.' He'd done his best. But he didn't have a clue what I was feeling. I should never have bothered him. As soon as he left I closed all the windows (it was a blazing hot day), curled up into a ball and howled.

Tilly, my King Charles spaniel, sat on my bed watching me in some amazement. Then, as my noisy sobbing went on, she got bored and tore off into the garden to chase something.

She's back now, licking my arms as I write this.

It's funny; I'm not actually ill, but my body aches as if I've got cramp. I suppose that's what complete misery does to you.

7.45 p.m.

Just when you think the day can't get any worse . . . Dad only went and repeated everything I told him in confidence to his woman friend (I refuse to call a fifty-four-year-old, a girl), Gloria.

I was so furious, even though I knew he meant well. The annoying thing is, that if Dad hadn't started losing his hair I really don't think he'd have bothered with Gloria at all.

After Mum died, Dad poured all his energy into his work. And five years went by without any significant lady friends. But then came the hair loss. And the wispier his hair, the more restless Dad became. Suddenly we moved to a bigger house – and Dad acquired a serious girlfriend: Gemma.

I really liked her. My aunts were shocked by the age difference (she was only twenty-nine), but I thought she was great: really good fun. However, that ended and then Dad brought home this alarmingly confident woman with stiff, white hair, who strode into our house as if she'd lived there all her life and announced to me, 'I know we're going to be great friends.'

But I knew at once we wouldn't be . . . and aren't. We haven't had any blazing rows or anything. We stay very much on the edges of each other's lives. Dad spends most of his time with Gloria at her house (she's a widow with no pesky children to get in the way) so we hardly see each other, which suits me just fine.

At six o'clock tonight, though, she sat beside me on the couch in the living room. I was still in my pyjamas – it was one of those days when you just don't see the point of getting dressed. She noticed this and gave a little frown of disapproval (what's the betting she's up at her desk every morning before five o'clock?). Then she patted my hand as if I were a troublesome three-year-old.

'First love, eh?' she said, and then gurgled with laughter as if she'd just made a joke. 'We all have to go through it, don't we?'

Dad stood in the doorway in his new crisp, red shirt and grey jeans (selected by guess who), nodding away at everything Gloria said.

'Yes, it can be difficult . . . first love,' she announced. 'Although I do think the word "love" is so over-used these days. Love is a word you have to grow into. But if ever you want to talk more about this –' then, looking across at Dad, she cooed – 'I'm a very good listener, aren't I?'

I thought Dad's head would fall off if he nodded any more enthusiastically.

'Thank you so much,' I said politely, 'but I'll be just fine.'

'Of course you will,' she practically shouted. Then, duty done, she swept off to go to the cinema with Dad. They had invited me – Dad even offered to let me choose the film – but I said I'd be OK here watching some DVDs with Tilly.

Dad – and certainly not Gloria – couldn't begin to understand the enormity of what had just happened to me.

As for all that patronizing tripe about first love. Well, for a start Luc wasn't my first love.

Dad's totally forgotten about this waiter I met on holiday in Spain with him last year. I noticed the waiter right away, although unfortunately he wasn't serving my table. But later he came up and waggled his ears at me. I laughed in surprise and admiration (he was an excellent ear-waggler). Then he told me his name – and a passionate week followed.

When we parted I cried a little because, despite everything he said, I realized I'd never hear from him again – and I haven't.

So, you see, I do know about relationships.

I don't fall in love very often, though. Unlike Andrea . . . every week there's a new boy who is totally 'fitilicious'.

One blond, tanned boy she was mad about worked in the local newsagent's in the evenings. So we were always in there on some pathetic excuse. Then he invited her to a mate's Christmas party. Of course, Andrea insisted I go with her.

There were far, far more boys at this party than girls. A gang of them were charging up and down the stairs, yelling. Another group were busy having a fight in the hallway. We pressed our way through them. For once, even Andrea was looking a bit apprehensive. Then the boy from the newsagent's swooped down on her and the two of them just vanished.

I was left knowing absolutely no one and feeling totally self-conscious. In the end I made for the kitchen. And then I noticed my nose had started running; it often does that when I get nervous. I crouched down and pretended to be looking into the fridge (it was, in fact, completely empty) while discreetly giving my nose a good blow.

It was then I heard a boy say, 'If you're hungry you can

have one of my peppermints.' So, yes, the very first time Luc saw me was when I was vigorously blowing my nose. Romantic or what?

'In fact, take two peppermints . . . you look hungry,' he went on. I hastily flung my hankie away and helped myself to two peppermints and took a better look at him.

He wasn't very tall (a shade smaller than me, in fact) and was dressed in a rather unflattering T-shirt and jeans. But he had exotic cheekbones and the most beautiful blue-green eyes imaginable. Oh yes, he was also wearing a tea cosy on his head. This made him look like a sensationally handsome pixie.

He leaned a bit closer to me. 'I don't normally model tea cosies but I got very bored.'

'That's when I reach for the tea cosy as well,' I replied.

He grinned at me. We'd been talking for less than a minute and already we were sharing a little joke. I'm not very at ease when I first meet new people – especially boys. It's one of my most irritating traits. Only this time there seemed to be a chemistry between us right away and I didn't feel an atom of shyness.

'I'm not bored any more,' he said, hurling the tea cosy away. 'I've seen you before, actually.'

'Oh, have you?' I said.

'Yes, I've watched you coming out of your school.'

The boys' school is just down the road from the girls' one. Only their school finishes fifteen minutes earlier than ours. This is supposed to discourage fraternization. Ha, ha, ha, and ho, ho, ho.

'You were with a group of other girls,' he went on. 'But I saw only you . . . I wanted to talk to you so much . . . though I'm sure lots of boys say that to you.'

'Oh yes, thousands,' I grinned.

'I can believe that,' he replied seriously. 'I'm Luc, by the way.'

'Hello, Luc . . . I'm Bella.'

He nodded as if I'd just told him something highly important.

We went on chatting away so easily. There was something very open about him and . . . well, I was going to add 'sweet', only I know Luc would absolutely hate to be described as that. Still, he'll never see this, will he? So, yes, he was 'sweet', but in the very best sense of the word. And he didn't seem at all self-conscious either as a lot of boys do. He just stood there, with his unruly, dark hair and eager smile and those wonderful mesmerizing eyes fixed on me – until the fight in the doorway spread right into the kitchen as well.

There was total chaos after that – at one point a television set even went flying out of the window – but I just managed to give Luc my mobile number before we were swept away from each other.

He called me the next day and I answered on the very first ring (dead uncool, I know, but I just couldn't wait).

We met for our first date under a leaden sky on Christmas Eve, and our last one – seven months later – on Tuesday 21 July. Now that was a total shock. I really thought Luc and me were sorted forever.

After school broke up, I went away for a few days with my dad. He wanted us to spend some 'quality time' together, but I sensed he missed Gloria a lot – and I certainly missed Luc like crazy.

So that meal together on 21 July was like my welcome back. Luc and I went to Pizza Paradiso, our favourite eating place (it's where teens go if they want something a bit more sophisticated than McDonald's and is really popular). I was so pleased to see Luc again, even if his eyes did look dead with tiredness. I thought he hasn't been sleeping well because he'd been missing me so much.

Little did I know . . . as they say.

I remember he was very subdued as well. I wondered if he'd had another argument with Patrick, his older brother. They're total opposites and don't get on at all. But then he declared, 'My mum's been having a right go at me.'

Something in his voice made me look up.

'What about?' I asked.

'About us, would you believe?' he whispered, peering down at his uneaten pizza. 'She thinks we're getting too serious too quickly.'

My scalp tightened. 'And what do you think?' I asked.

His reply was so quiet I had to lean forward to hear him. 'I think, maybe, we should cool it for a while – yes.'

For a moment I was so stunned that everything – including Luc – went totally out of focus. It was the oddest sensation. Then, from another part of the room came a huge roar of laughter, followed by loud clapping. All around me was this great sea of happiness, while my world had just been blown sky-high.

I wasn't merely happy with Luc, I was totally blissed out. Surely I'd have sensed if something was wrong between us? Of course I would. I couldn't be that insensitive.

So, I decided, whatever's gone wrong can still be sorted. Luc doesn't really want to finish with me. I have to be calm and find out what's really happened.

'Luc, we're not breaking up because of your mum . . . there isn't someone else, is there?' I asked softly, fully expecting him to say, 'Of course not,' and being cross with me for even suggesting such a thing.

So his reply came as a violent shock. 'Yes, Bella, I'm afraid there is,' he whispered, and a great wave of colour rushed into his face. It was all too much to take in. I could hardly speak. Tears welled up at the corners of my eyes.

After a long, silent moment Luc said, still gazing at his pizza, 'I promise you, Bella, I do care about you. I still want us to be friends.'

Suddenly my feelings swerved towards anger. 'So who is it?' I demanded, in a kind of screaming whisper. 'No, don't tell me, I don't want her name polluting my head.' I scrambled to my feet. Luc raised startled eyes at me, but what was he expecting? After news like that I couldn't go on sitting there, happily munching my pizza.

I cried out, 'PLEASE, PLEASE, PLEASE don't come after me, it'll only make everything much worse. Have a nice life, won't you?'

Then I pelted out of there and straight off to Andrea's. She couldn't have been more understanding. The following afternoon I was round her house again.

And now I did want to know who had stolen Luc from me. But when I asked Andrea she didn't rattle off a list of suspects as I'd expected. She just shrugged and said she hadn't a clue. I thought that was a bit unusual but I decided she must have been sparing my feelings.

In the evening Dad and me were supposed to be visiting my Aunt Libby in Bedford. She had the flu, though, so I shot round to see Andrea again . . . and that's when I sighted them, standing outside her house.

Want to know my very first thought? What a top friend I've got. She's trying to sort things out for me with Luc. My heart actually swelled with gratitude – until I watched the longest kiss I'd ever seen. After which I heard Luc say, 'You must tell her soon.'

And 'her' had never suspected Andrea for a moment. I knew she was something of a 'boy trap' – but I really thought her best friend's boyfriend was off limits. In fact, now I think about it, I even asked her to keep an eye on Luc for me while I was on holiday . . .

But it won't last. That's my one consolation. Andrea gets through boyfriends so quickly – poor Luc won't know what's hit him.

Poor Luc – now you're thinking that's an odd thing to write. After all, he's just as guilty as Andrea. Of course he is. And I'm so disappointed in him. But boys haven't got the same strength of character as girls. That's a scientific fact. And they can be very easily distracted, if you know what I mean.

That's what's happened here. Luc's been temporarily distracted by my best friend.

This is just a blip. I say that to myself over and over. And I give Luc and Andrea a week – at the most!!

So I shall have the last laugh when they both come crawling back to me. What a moment that will be – and all this misery will then instantly slip away.

I'VE JUST GOT TO WAIT.

Chapter 3

SATURDAY 25 JULY

Email to Bella

Dear Bella,

First of all, I totally forgive you for destroying my dress. In your situation I'm sure I'd have done exactly the same — no worse, much worse.

I know exactly how very hurt you must be. Believe me, it's the last thing Luc or me wanted. Believe me, too, this is not a silly flirtation. And when you were away we just couldn't hide our strong feelings any more. We really did try, but it was impossible. One day, I hope I can explain all this to you.

Right now it just seems so very strange without you. You should be here with me, celebrating my birthday. But Bella, whenever you want to meet I'll be there. Your friendship means the world to me. Always remember that.

Lots of love,

Andrea XXX

6.00 p.m.

SHE FORGIVES ME!!

The nerve of her! As for all that gush about her and Luc and their strong feelings for each other . . . I'm amazed I wasn't sick all over my computer.

Andrea forgets I know her. I've lost count of all her silly crushes. Well, there's a new one practically every week. My boyfriend just happens to be the latest one. But she and Luc haven't been deeply attracted for ages. That's a total lie. I'd have realized. I'd have sensed Luc slipping away from me. No, she made a big play for my boyfriend when I was safely away.

As for all that syrupy rubbish about my friendship meaning the world to her – oh yes, it really looks like it, doesn't it?

I so wish she hadn't contacted me. It's just stirred me up again. I've been pacing around the house (Dad, of course, is at Gloria's tonight), with Tilly flying after me and barking excitedly; obviously thinking this is some new kind of game.

Too upset to write any more right now.

9.00 p.m.

I've just been sitting in a bus shelter. I wasn't waiting for a bus, though. No, nothing as normal as that.

The bus shelter, you see, is directly opposite Andrea's house. And I've been slouched in the corner, squinting through my sunglasses (that's my disguise) at the guests arriving for Andrea's party. Exactly why I'd want to do this I can't tell you. It's a complete mystery even to me.

19

So I watched this flash car pull up and a girl flounce out – Lydia. She's in my class at school and she and Andrea are always gossiping together. Lydia and I are rather less friendly.

The front door opened and Andrea gave a little squeal of delight when she saw Lydia. Then she grabbed her by the arm and half-dragged her into the house. I noticed Andrea was wearing a new black dress. No doubt that had been bought specially for her today. She'd had her hair done, too: new dress, new hairstyle – new boyfriend.

I should have left then. I mean, what on earth was the point of watching all this? Was my life so small and pointless that I couldn't think of anything else to do?

'GO NOW!'

In my head I shouted this advice, but I still ignored it. Clearly I wasn't quite miserable enough yet. I had to drain my cup of poison by watching him arrive . . .

I didn't have long to wait.

And then I just couldn't believe it. It still seemed so unreal to me. It was like watching a stranger wearing a mask of Luc, kissing Andrea. And they both looked so happy together while here I was, skulking across the road like the Ghost of Christmas Past.

I shot to my feet, flooded with pain. All right, I'd show them. I'd storm into that party now; ruin a few minutes of it, at least. And if I was very lucky I might even sabotage the whole evening. I hadn't a clue what I was going to say – but no doubt inspiration would come to me at the right moment.

I just wanted to wipe that smug smile right off Andrea's face.

I was about to charge across the road to do exactly that when I heard someone call my name. I looked around sharply. And there was this boy I'd never in my life seen before. He just seemed to materialize out of nowhere.

He strolled over to me with such a friendly expression on his face, as if we'd known each other for years.

'Really not a good idea, you know,' he said.

I could only gape at him.

'You were intending to gatecrash that party, weren't you, Bella?'

'How exactly do you know my name?' My voice sounded shrill and scared.

He just grinned. He was wearing a cool blue suit with a very loose tie and white trainers. He was about eighteen, tall and not bad-looking, I suppose. And he had that air of confidence and assurance that people who are about to sell you something often assume.

A horrible thought struck me. Andrea's got a cousin. I'd never met him, but he was coming to her party – and he was about eighteen. Hadn't Andrea also said he was going to act as her bodyguard? She must have guessed I'd turn up tonight and assigned him the job of keeping me out. What was his name? Barry, that's it.

'Is your name Barry?' I asked fiercely.

He smiled and said, 'No.'

'Are you sure?'

'I think that's something I would remember.' He grinned again.

'So what is it?' I demanded.

'Rupert, but that's really not important,' he said. 'How about if we stroll into town? . . . There's a café there . . .'

'No, no,' I burst out. He couldn't just pop up and 'pick me up'. I wasn't that desperate.

He immediately raised a hand. 'That was only a suggestion . . . and now you look highly alarmed, which is the very last thing I intended. I shouldn't have just jumped out at you, either – I always get that introductory bit wrong. Now look,' he dug into his pocket, 'here's my card. At least take that. Please.' He reached out his hand to me. I snatched up the card.

'Thank you,' he said. 'And I would strongly advise you to call me.'

'Oh, would you?'

'I'd also strongly advise you not to go to that party. I know how tempting it is. It's what I'd want to do in your situation. But you'll only make yourself look undignified . . . and very forlorn. You've got to stay away.'

'Just how exactly do you know all about this?' I cried. 'I've never seen you in my life.'

'Call me and you'll find out,' he said cheerfully. 'Ring me any time, day or night. I offer a twenty-four-hour listening service.'

Across the road more cars were pulling up; there were excited whoops and screams, too. He moved forward.

'Don't even look at them, Bella,' he urged. 'Just get right away from here and go home now.'

So here was a total stranger, appearing out of nowhere and showering me with advice. What a nerve! Yet, some part of me knew it was good advice.

'Well, perhaps I will leave,' I announced.

'Well done!' he cried and looked genuinely pleased. 'We'll talk again very soon.'

He said this with such confidence, too.

I started walking away. When I turned around I expected to see him still standing by the bus shelter. But he'd vanished as mysteriously as he'd appeared.

For one crazy moment I even wondered if he was some sort of ghost: the ghost of the bus shelter, who hands out advice to miserable souls.

Now I was just being daft. And hadn't he given me a card? Well, ghosts certainly don't go around doing that, do they?

I took off my sunglasses and studied the card he'd given me. It just had his name on it and underneath, 'The Ex-Files', followed by a mobile number.

I'd heard of *The X-Files*, of course: that TV series about investigations into spooky happenings. But not the Ex-Files.

He was clearly a very odd person: kind of compelling while he was talking to you, though.

And now I could see that he had done me a good turn. Barging into Andrea's party might well have provided some drama and given everyone a wonderful gossip afterwards, but it really wouldn't have helped me.

I'd have just degraded myself – and right in front of Luc as well.

Now I kept looking at that Ex-Files card, wondering what would happen if I actually called that number.

Not that I ever would, of course.

Chapter 4

SUNDAY 26 JULY

I'm in disgrace.

What happened was: well, first of all I hardly slept last night. My head was too full of thoughts and wild imaginings. I'd hear the clock downstairs chiming two o'clock, three o'clock, four o'clock, and each time the chimes sounded more surprised, as if they couldn't believe I was still awake. And there was that weird kind of stillness, as if the whole world was under glass. I finally drifted off about half past four, but was awake again before seven.

So when Dad returned at about half past ten this morning from his time with Gloria I was slumped on the couch, still in my pyjamas, gazing foggily at some teen soap on television.

To my great surprise and alarm, I also heard Gloria's voice in the hallway – she never comes back with Dad. The next thing I knew she was standing right in front of me, sighing deeply and exclaiming, 'This won't do, will it?'

'It really won't,' agreed Dad, gently smiling.

Gloria was wearing a brightly coloured turban. It was so dazzling it seemed to assault my eyes every time I dared to glance at it. She placed a hand on mine. I peered down at the freshly polished nails; she always makes me feel so shabby.

'My god-daughter, Rosemary, is visiting me for lunch today. You've heard me mention her?'

I had, many times.

'Well, she'd love to meet you and we won't accept "No" for an answer. So, do you want any help getting dressed?' She was talking to me in exaggeratedly sympathetic tones now. I really didn't want her helping me get dressed. In fact, the horror of that image got me to my feet and up the stairs straightaway.

I had no wish to have lunch with Gloria or her paragon of a god-daughter either. But I told myself to be patient: Gloria meant well and it would please Dad (and that, of course, was Gloria's main reason for inviting me).

Dad was waiting for me at the bottom of the stairs. 'Now, that's more like the Bella I know,' he said. 'Scrubs up well, doesn't she, Gloria?'

Gloria beamed at me. 'We must have a good girly chat about make-up and clothes one day: exchange tips.'

I could hardly wait.

Her flat was tiny but immaculate. I felt very self-conscious, especially when I saw all the expensive dishes and plates. It seemed a bit over the top for a chicken salad.

For once it wasn't Gloria who did all of the talking.

Rosemary chatted on and on about her holiday in America, her gap year, her new home and a national handwriting prize she'd won . . . She also had no interest in me whatsoever. I wasn't sure she totally approved of Dad, either. She kept giving him these strange glances and addressed all her conversation to Gloria.

We seemed to have been sitting at that table for twenty years, and still Rosemary was holding forth. I felt my eyes drooping. And quite suddenly, and very shockingly, I slumped forward and fell asleep.

It was Dad calling my name who made me jump awake again. I stared blearily around, uncertain exactly where I was for a moment. I spotted Gloria first, sitting very upright and looking as if she was chewing a wasp.

When we were leaving I did apologize to her. I said, 'Sorry for falling asleep like that. It's no offence to you. I'm just so tired.' Gloria laughed softly, but her face was all hard and closed in on itself.

Back home there was a definite chill in the atmosphere. Dad never says much; he's not one for conflicts or arguments (although he does sulk). Suddenly he said to me, 'Are you still missing that boy?' There was a note of incredulity in his voice, as if he couldn't believe I hadn't got over Luc. I'd had four whole days, for goodness' sake.

'Maybe,' he went on, 'you should go and stay with . . .' I never let him finish that sentence. I get on really well with my Aunt Libby, but I wouldn't let him parcel me off there now. It was imperative that I was here, ready for when Luc came back to me.

'I don't want to go anywhere right now,' I said, firmly. 'Don't worry, I'll be fine.'

Dad stared at me anxiously. 'You must try and get a grip on things,' he said, and then added, a bit more kindly, 'And just relax more . . . I'd love to have another five weeks of summer holiday stretching ahead of me. Don't waste these precious days . . . One day, you know, you'll look back on this break-up and realize how totally unimportant it was.'

'No, I'll never, ever do that,' I replied, but I waited until Dad was out of the room before I said it.

MONDAY 27 JULY
4.00 p.m.

A brilliant thing has just happened: Lydia's rung me.

Now you're puzzled. Especially if you remember me telling you that Lydia and I are not especially good friends. In fact, we merely tolerate each other because of our friendship (now deceased, in my case) with Andrea.

So why should a call from Lydia cause me such deep joy?

I'll tell you why: Lydia said she'd missed me at the party on Saturday and wanted to see how I was. Well, I nearly laughed out loud. Lydia didn't have a splinter of concern for me. She was ringing for just one reason: Andrea had put her up to it.

Then – ever so casually – Lydia asked me if I'd heard from Luc at all. At once I knew this was the real reason for the call. But why does Andrea want to know this? Have she and Luc argued already? (Andrea's got a mean temper. It comes from being so spoilt.) Could Luc be starting to lose interest in her? Does he realize that he's made a catastrophic mistake?

The questions whirled round and round in my head, making me feel quite dizzy. I told myself I mustn't get too excited. Still, this wild hope rose up: Luc and I were about to be reunited.

I always knew Luc and Andrea wouldn't last: they were all wrong together. But even I never expected them to break up this fast.

Now Andrea's absolutely terrified Luc is going to ring me and ask if I'll take him back. In fact, when Luc does ring I shan't say 'Yes' to him right away. I do have some pride. I'll make him wait two or three minutes at least.

But I also realize this was only a blip and afterwards Luc and I will be stronger than ever. My friendship with Andrea is another matter entirely. I just don't think I could ever trust her again. So, shortly Andrea will lose both Luc and me. I can't feel sorry for her, though. Not yet, anyway.

Now all I have to do is wait for Luc to contact me.

8.00 p.m.

Luc hasn't called yet.

And I've been waiting for him so eagerly; must have practised in my head what I'm going to say to him a thousand times. I'm like an actress who's rehearsed her part so frequently she just wants to tear on to the stage and perform her role.

Then I wondered if Luc might send me an email, so I've been checking those very regularly. But Luc isn't a great sender of emails. No, I'm sure he'll ring. I've just got to be patient.

10.30 p.m.

Too late for Luc to ring now, but I've got my mobile by my bed just in case. Have a horrible feeling he's too ashamed to call me. Too embarrassed, as well. If only I could somehow let him know that I won't give him a hard time.

12.00 midnight

Inspiration has just hit me. Now I know what to do.

TUESDAY 28 JULY
10.15 a.m.

It had seemed such a brilliant idea last night. But it's lost most of its lustre in the bright morning light.

I'm standing just outside this sports shop, where Patrick (Luc's brother) works. My plan was/is to breeze in there, chat casually with Patrick about this and that, then slip in my little message to Luc at the end.

It seemed so easy. Now all these doubts are crowding in.

For a start, Luc and Patrick don't really get on. So is Patrick really the right person to deliver my friendly words? And what if he deliberately gets my message wrong to stir things up?

Maybe I should just abandon the whole idea. But I really don't want to do that either. I almost wish that boy I saw on Saturday at the bus stop would suddenly appear again – and advise me. Mind you, he'd probably tell me to forget the whole thing. And I know that's what I should do.

But, on the other hand, all I'm doing is strolling around a shop and bumping into Luc's brother totally 'by accident'. Where's the harm in that? And to be honest, all this waiting around is killing me. I've got to do something.

10.35 a.m.

Well, I did it.

An assistant was standing in the doorway of the sports shop, arguing loudly with a group of other boys. 'No way, I'm not having that,' he cried. Then he spotted me squeezing past. 'All right?' he barked and immediately resumed his argument.

He seemed more like a bouncer really, allowing me into an exclusive club. Music was blaring out too, but the place was completely empty, save for two assistants at the back of the shop lacing up trainers. One of whom was Patrick.

But I didn't rush over there, no, far too obvious. Instead, I examined a few tracksuits in a highly interested sort of way and then stared keenly about me, like an explorer in new territory (and I'd never, ever been in here before, although I'd passed it many times).

Finally, and very slowly, I eased my way over to the trainers section. Patrick was saying, 'I'm telling you, man, that's what she said to me. No exaggeration.'

The red-haired boy he was with sniggered. 'Dream on,' he said.

Patrick looks a bit like Luc, only he's bigger, with hooded eyes and much more attitude.

'Oh, hey, Patrick!' I cried, hoping I wasn't overdoing my surprise at spotting him. 'I totally forgot you worked in here.'

'Hello,' he replied, adding, after a slight pause, 'Bella! So what are you looking for?'

'Oh, nothing in particular . . . just looking.' And as this sounded a bit feeble, I added, 'Your prices seem very reasonable compared to other sports shops I've been visiting today. I'm going round them all, trying to get the best bargains. It's taking me ages.' I laughed.

He didn't smile back. Instead, he went on scrutinizing me as if I were some very rare creature he'd just discovered. 'Never seen you in here before,' he muttered at last.

'Oh, really, haven't you?' I said as lightly as I could. 'No, I pop in here from time to time. Got a great atmosphere, hasn't it?' He didn't answer. There was a thick smell of foam and plastic which made me feel a bit sick. And Patrick was still watching me very curiously. I was sure he'd guessed why I'd accidentally met him. But I mustn't blush or get nervous. I just had to say what I'd practised. I edged nearer. I took a deep breath. I had no idea this would feel so undignified.

'Actually, Patrick, I was wondering how Luc is.' I stopped there, hoping the red-haired boy would recognize this was now a private conversation and leave us, but he didn't move a muscle. Patrick didn't say anything at first either, just studied me from underneath his lowered eyelids.

At last he said, 'Wouldn't know . . . hardly ever see him.' This wasn't promising at all. In fact, it was excruciating. But I ploughed on. 'Well, next time you see Luc I wonder if you'd do me a favour and give him a little message from me?' Again, no response at all. 'Would you just . . . say hi from me and tell him to give me a call if he wants to?' I stopped and gave a nervous little laugh. 'Do you want to write that down?' I asked.

'No, I'll remember it,' he replied, in a funny, muffled voice. I had a horrible feeling he wanted to laugh.

'Thanks a lot then, Patrick,' I cried. 'And see you soon, maybe . . . and, well, bye.'

Then I sprang off, walking straight into a display of football shirts. As I was leaving I heard Patrick say in a piercing whisper, 'No, she's not the girl I was telling you about.' He laughed sharply at the very idea. 'That's my brother's ex.'

But not for much longer! As, by tonight, Luc will have got my message (I really wish Patrick had written it down) and will know it's all right to ring, because I'm ready to forgive and forget. And that truly, ghastly little scene will have been worthwhile.

10.20 p.m.

He never rang.

But he must have received my message by now. Unless Patrick forgot all about it. That's possible, isn't it? Or maybe Patrick didn't deliver it in the right way.

Now what should I do? Go on waiting for Luc to pluck up the courage to ring me? But all this waiting really gets you down, you know, and the thought of more endless days like this one . . . I don't know if I can stand it.

WEDNESDAY 29 JULY
6.45 p.m.

I've spoken to Luc!

He didn't call me, though. I just couldn't wait any longer, so I rang him. I was going to send off a friendly email but then decided a phone call would be much better. And I wanted to hear Luc's voice so badly.

It would be a very bright chat. I'd just cheerily enquire as to how he was. Nothing heavy at all. But Luc would know I was ready to . . . well, start things up again.

His mobile was switched off so then I called his house. I might get his mum but that's all right. She'd always liked me and I would be very cheerful. As I dialled the number, Tilly – who was sitting on my bed beside me – started thumping her tail, just as if she knew something momentous was about to happen.

I waited for someone to reply, with one arm tightly around Tilly, and absolutely sick with nerves.

'Hello.'

Just hearing Luc's voice gave me a little shiver. 'Hi, it's me, Bella.' There was a moment of complete silence as if he were remembering me from a long way back.

Then he said, 'Hello, Bella . . . are you all right?' His voice sounded so strange, all muffled and low. He thinks

I've rung to have a go at him. I must show him I'm not going to do that.

So I said, breezily, 'Oh, I'm just fine and Tilly's with me. She sends you one of her sloppy licks.' I stopped. This was the moment he should say how much he missed me. He'd said it in my head absolutely hundreds of times, so it was quite a shock not hearing him say it now. Instead, all I could hear was the downstairs clock ticking away in the silence.

'I don't know if Patrick gave you my message,' I cried at last.

'Yes, he did,' replied Luc, and his voice was so flat, so totally expressionless, I knew I should ring off right now while I'd still got a tiny shred of dignity left. Instead, I clung tightly on to the phone. An icy sweat broke out on my forehead.

I started burbling. 'It was such a surprise to see Patrick today, I'd totally forgotten he worked there and –'

'Actually, I'm really sorry,' interrupted Luc, 'but I'm just on my way out now.'

That was a lie, wasn't it? He wanted to end this grisly conversation. Or maybe he really was off to see her: Andrea.

'Well, thanks for calling.' He said this so formally it caught me under my heart. Up to a week ago I was his girlfriend, his soulmate. Now he was talking to me as if I were someone he hardly knew. And I couldn't reply. I just let out this little sob, which I really hope he didn't hear.

But he definitely heard these next words, which just

tumbled out. 'Before you go, Luc, tell me this one thing. What did I do wrong?'

'You didn't do anything wrong,' he replied at once. 'It's just a very bad situation for all of us, but especially for you. I'm sincerely sorry for it all.' His voice cracked suddenly. 'That's all I can say right now –' and he rang off.

I got up, my face burning with shame. How could I have misread things so completely? Luc wasn't breaking up with Andrea at all. And the very last person he wanted to talk to was me.

As soon as I heard his tone I knew that call was a huge mistake. Why didn't I ring off then? Instead, I had to ask him what I'd done wrong; that made me sound so needy (which boys hate), and a bit freaky as well.

The problem is, I just can't understand how someone can shower you with little gifts and cards with messages on them like, 'You mean the whole world to me,' and then, hey presto, it's over and they don't even want to talk to you on the phone after that.

You can't just switch off the way you feel about someone, as if you were extinguishing a light. Only, apparently, you can.

I just wish someone would teach me how to do it.

7.40 p.m.

I told Dad I was going round to see a friend. But guess where I really am – that's right, at that bus stop again!

'But what on earth's the point of doing that?' is the

36

question you're screaming at me. Well, I've decided to just squeeze out a few extra drops of despair by hanging around here once more. Any minute now I may even see Andrea and Luc all loved up together . . . just to give my evening that extra kick.

I SHOULD GO HOME. I do realize that. But somehow I can't. This was where I first saw Luc and my best friend together and I suppose I still haven't got over it. That's why I'm returning here again. I just don't know what else to do.

Anyway, without Luc, nothing in my life makes any sense.

Tears have started swimming in my eyes now. I shall break down in a minute. No, please don't let me do that opposite Andrea's house. At least let me have a break-down in the privacy of my own bedroom. Only I can't even do that, because Dad is back home and he'd be very alarmed if I cracked up. He might even send for Gloria! So it looks as if there's nothing else for it. I'll just have to delay my breakdown until tomorrow morning when he's gone to work.

I try to smile but I can't quite manage it. I feel so completely lonely and mixed up and totally lost. I suddenly think about my mum. She passed away more than six years ago now and Dad and I hardly ever mention her. She's vanished from everywhere, except my bedroom wall. She still looks down on me from there. She was such a positive, dynamic person. I really wish she were here now. She'd put me right. Suddenly I miss her more than I have for ages and ages.

Then I start looking around for that boy I met here on Saturday. I have a feeling he might turn up again tonight. I almost want him to, to tell the truth.

And for the millionth time I look at that Ex-Files card and wonder about calling him. I've done so many stupid things these past days. Will it really matter if I do just one more? And surely anything's better than skulking around here.

7.55 p.m.

I rang him. He didn't sound at all surprised to hear from me either. In fact, I really think he'd been expecting my call. He told me I wasn't to move and he'd be with me very shortly.

So I'm just sitting here waiting . . . I've had so much practice at doing that, these past few days. And also . . . Wait, I can hear footsteps. Can't be him already. I think it is . . . Got to stop now.

DANNY'S STORY

Chapter 5

MONDAY 27 JULY

I thought I was going to spend tonight in a police cell. Everything just kicked off this evening

It started with me storming up to Nicole's house and yelling at her through a traffic cone. (It was the nearest thing I could find to a megaphone.)

I didn't shout anything really bad; mainly I just asked her to talk to me. And if she'd done that her dad wouldn't have needed to appear – eyes popping out of his head – and he and I wouldn't have had that massive row.

And then this police car pulled up. I really thought they'd have had better things to do. I was only shouting, that's all. I wasn't smashing anything up.

The two policemen spoke to me dead quietly. I suppose this was to calm me down. Then they asked me to come with them. I was scared they were going to arrest me. But they didn't. They just wanted me to put the traffic cone back where I'd found it, and gave me a police escort while I did this. They then left. That was a massive relief.

But I've realized I sank to my very lowest tonight. These past few days Nicole had got me so pumped up with frustration, and tonight . . . well, I came into her life out of nowhere, and it really looks as if I'm going straight back there now.

So what was I? Her bit of rough? Her walk on the wild side?

And how did we exactly get here? I keep trying to figure that out.

Let's just rewind things to six weeks ago when we met for the very first time in the town centre. I'll always remember what Nicole's friend, James, whispered to her: 'I see the Chavs are out in force tonight,' and with such stinging contempt as if Chavs were carriers of some highly infectious disease – and best kept right away from.

I suppose I'm a Chav. Well, I go around with this pack of boys at night and, shock, horror, we wear black hoodies (hoodies are really just sweatshirts with an extra bit . . . never understood all the fuss about them). And we do wild and crazy things, like all walk into a shop together and knock a packet of biscuits over. We like to think we're gangsters!!

But I'd say I'm about fifteen or twenty other people also. And one of them is this dead romantic guy. That's not something I advertise, but yes, I believe out there somewhere is this special person who you are just destined to be with.

Gary used to laugh when I went on about this, but I think he sort of believed it, too.

Anyway, this particular night I was out with my fellow

hoodies when I saw this sensational-looking girl walk quickly past with a skinny geezer. She could have been a model she was so beautiful. And I had no idea she was only fourteen, the same age as me. If someone had said she was twenty I'd have believed it. Anyway, without even quite realizing it, I smiled, and she gave me a little, teasing smile right back. We definitely had a moment there. Then she walked on and I whispered to Gary, 'I think I've found her, my dream girl.'

And Gary said, 'Well, go after her, you muppet. Don't let her get away.' So I did just that. I tore over and yelled, 'Fat penguin.'

She turned round, looking a bit startled until I quickly added, 'Now we've broken the ice . . . I'm Danny, by the way, and I just had to say you look totally beautiful.'

The girl grinned at me and replied, 'Hello, Danny, I'm Nicole.' Straightaway she told me her name – I liked that.

And so many cosmic feelings were flowing between us until that guy she was with (James, as I later found out) muttered that line about the Chavs being out in force, and practically pushed her away from me. And that was it.

Gary said I should go after her and get her phone number. I replied, 'This isn't the right time, but I'll see her again.' I really believed that, you know. Every night I scanned the town searching for Nicole and a week later, we did meet again.

I was only with Gary this time and we were hanging about as usual by the fountain when I sighted her. She was sitting with James on one of the benches. Beside her was this great pile of books.

'She's a big reader all right,' commented Gary.

A couple of times Nicole glanced in my direction. We weren't very far away and I'm sure she saw me. But she seemed a bit shy and embarrassed. Funnily enough, that's exactly how I felt. Gary was urging me to go over but I kept hesitating.

Then Nicole got up, picking up all her books – except one, which she'd obviously forgotten. I charged after her, waving that book.

'I think you left this behind, Nicole,' I said. James immediately groaned as if I'd done something very stupid.

'Just put it back,' he snarled.

'What's his problem?' I said to Nicole.

She replied softly. 'I don't suppose you've heard of "book-crossing"?'

'No . . . I've heard of books, though.'

Nicole laughed. 'Actually, hardly anyone has heard of book-crossing yet. It's where a group of people pick a book they think is really good. Then they get as many second-hand copies as they can find and release these copies into railway stations and cafés and on to benches –'

'For other people to find and read,' I interrupted.

'That's it.' Then she asked, with a smile, 'And you think we're completely mad?'

'Of course he does,' said James as he snatched the book out of my hand and put it back on the bench.

Before I could say another word he was hustling Nicole away. But she called over to me, 'This month's book-crossing title was chosen by me – it's my all-time favourite.'

It wasn't until later I realized the significance of what she had just told me.

When I explained to Gary what Nicole had been doing he was disgusted. 'She can't have much of a social life if she just goes around at night putting books everywhere.' He added, 'No way is that uncool weirdo your dream girl.'

I pretended to go along with him, too. Funny how you're often less truthful with your mates than anyone else.

And I suppose what she was doing was a bit strange. But you can have 'good strange', too – and to me, book-crossing was definitely in that category.

After I left Gary I slipped back to the bench, hoping like crazy that Nicole's book would still be there. And it was. Just inside it was this card, which said, 'TAKE ME HOME AND READ ME'.

The book was dead old; there were even little grey spots on some of its pages, but it was exciting to think I was reading Nicole's all-time favourite story. It was as if I was getting to know her dead intimately right away.

The book was called *I Capture the Castle* by Dodie Smith. It's about a girl called Cassandra, who, I thought, would be dead posh when I read her name and found out she lived in a castle. Only the castle's a bit of a ruin and her relations are pretty mad and she hasn't got any money.

And I really liked it because everything was so well described. Cassandra's quite a laugh, too. I think I'd have got on with her.

Anyway, I devoured it in three days. At the end of the book there was a website where you could log on your comments about the book. And scrawled underneath was a phone number you could also ring. Later, of course, Nicole told me that only one copy of *I Capture the Castle* had a phone number in it. She had scribbled it in, hoping I'd come back and take the book. I thought that was very romantic when I found out.

Of course, I did call Nicole. And at first she asked me all these questions about the book. She was laughing as she did so but I think she wanted to check I'd actually read it. It was as if she'd set me a challenge. Anyway, I passed with flying colours. We even had a friendly argument about the ending. I wanted a happier one, with everything sorted out, but Nicole liked it only being sort of happy, because it made her keep thinking about the characters.

Then my heart gave a massive thump as I asked her if she was doing anything tomorrow. She said she was – she belonged to this group called Teens Take Action who'd organized the book-crossing. They also discussed issues of the day . . . maybe I'd like to come along to their next meeting at Colby's Bookshop.

I was so chuffed that she'd asked me, even though I knew exactly what my mates would say – going to Teens Take Action was nothing less than social suicide! Also, I realized I wasn't exactly a typical member of Teens Take Action. But none of that bothered me. Knowing Nicole wanted me there made me feel so high, as if I could do anything. So I said 'Yes' right away. Then I thought, *How lucky am I? I'm just fourteen years old – yet I've met my soulmate already.*

Writing that now makes me feel so depressed and angry that I'm going to pause here and do something very stupid.

Chapter 6

TUESDAY 28 JULY
12.50 a.m.

I'm back – but not before . . .

I've just made a nuisance call, haven't I? – to James.

I called him up on his mobile, about five minutes ago. Nicole was always ringing James, so I knew his number. This voice, fogged with sleep, answered.

'Your days are numbered,' I hissed.

'What?' he spluttered. I could almost taste his fear.

'Just to let you know you're going to die soon. Bye.'

Then I rang off. I thought he might call me back, but he hasn't. Too scared, I expect.

I blame James for just about everything that's gone wrong between Nicole and me.

I'll start with that Teens Take Action meeting.

I arrived there quite late – because of nerves, I'm afraid. Inside Colby's Bookshop I saw seven teenagers sat round in a semicircle between the 'New Age' and 'Gardening' sections. A man with the smallest, gingeriest beard I've ever seen bounded over to me. 'Ah, new blood, excellent.'

Everyone – apart from Nicole – stared at me as if I'd just wandered in from another planet. I found out later they all went to the same school for aspiring twits. That's what we call it, anyway.

I swaggered over to a seat but I was shaking inside. Then Nicole smiled at me and whispered, 'So glad you could make it,' as if she really meant it.

I noticed she was sitting with James and looked so pally with him that a chill ran through me. Was he actually her boyfriend? I had to find out.

I did make one attempt at grinning at James. Only he didn't react at all, just went on sitting there, face like a tombstone. He's got one of those very long faces with a tight, little mouth, permanently furrowed brow and breath that smells like old underpants. All right, I'm exaggerating now, but he only has to enter a room to suck all the oxygen out of it.

Then he stood up to deliver his speech and it was on the subject of – hoodies. I was only wearing jeans and a T-shirt that night but he looked right at me when he announced his topic.

'They might seem just like pathetic fashion victims,' he said, 'but they're not, they're morons, as well.' He gave me another piercing glare as he said the word 'morons'. And I noticed Nicole glance at me anxiously, but I kept my face totally expressionless.

'Every night these street boys, as they like to call themselves, leave their ugly mark on this town . . .'

Well, he ranted for ages like that. It was as if he were challenging me to a fight – only with words, not fists.

So, after he'd finished I stood up and we faced each other like two gladiators. Then I announcd, 'There're a few more things you might not know about hoodies,' and I just told a few funny stories about daft things we'd done. Well, they went down a storm. Everyone was killing themselves laughing, except for James, of course.

At the end I got this massive round of applause. And I think that made Nicole see me in a whole new light. 'I'm so proud of you,' she said afterwards, just as if I were her new discovery.

Everyone else (with one exception) was clustering round me, too. Suddenly, all these posh, intellectual types wanted to be in with me – hilarious, really.

Then I said to Nicole, 'It's getting dark outside and you might get attacked by lions. So may I have the honour of walking you home . . . alone?'

We left James glowering at us and I felt so triumphant.

On the way home Nicole apologized for him. 'When he was younger he got picked on all the time by a gang of loud, massively confident boys . . . and I think you remind him of them.'

'That's nice to know,' I muttered.

She laughed. 'He takes a while to trust people, but when he does he's so great. And in the end I think you and James will become very good friends.'

I raised two sceptical eyebrows.

She added, 'He's my very best friend.' So I never said

another word about him that night. Instead, I asked her out on a date.

Nicole gave me her cheeky, teasing smile. 'So where are you going to take me?' It was as if she were setting me another challenge.

Then I had a brainwave. Thanks to Gary's cousin, I'd managed to get tickets to see the Atomic Freaks, our only famous local band. Nicole was very impressed by that, as I remember.

The night we saw the Atomic Freaks they just went nuts on stage. Everyone was swept away by them, including us . . . We were having a brilliant time until Nicole spotted James there with two other girls from Teens Take Action.

So, somehow James had managed to get tickets as well. That certainly drained the night of some of its magic. But I was determined to forget about him and at the interval Nicole and I were having such a laugh together, until he announced, 'I'm going home now, Nicole.' His words fell on us like a shadow; he stood there, just loaded with misery. I knew the Atomic Freaks wouldn't be to his taste, so what on earth was he doing here, anyway?

Nicole went off with him, though. 'He seems very upset about something,' she murmured back to me. 'I won't be long.' But she was gone ages. And yes, I was angry. She was on a date with me, not him. This was our evening together.

Later I introduced Nicole to Gary, whose opening remark to her was, 'Read any good books lately?' He was just trying to be funny but she wasn't very amused.

Afterwards this terrible feeling of hopelessness hit me.

There was no denying James was allergic to me. Meanwhile, in the other corner, there were my mates who thought she was 'stuck up' and called me 'Nicole's little puppy dog'. But then, I figured, what did any of that matter. The only important thing was that we'd fallen for each other.

And knowing Nicole was in my life meant every bit of my day – even the grey, grinding parts – had this extra beat of happiness in it. Even so, I couldn't quite believe I'd be able to pull a girl like her. Now I had to keep her with me. And the pressure was on, big style.

When it was only Nicole and me, we got on so well. I remember one time we left a party early because we didn't have eyes for anyone except each other. The atmosphere between us was just electric that night. If only we could have lived in a little bubble, Nicole and me: no one else. But we couldn't. Other people kept pushing their way in, like James.

Always James.

That night in Pizza Paradiso when Nicole told me he would be going on holiday with her and her family . . . well, I was speechless with shock at first.

'Why?' I asked at last.

She laughed softly. 'Why? Because James came with my family last year and he shared a room with my cousin and they get on really well. So he's doing just the same this year . . . It's only a week and it's no big deal, Danny, honestly.' And perhaps it wouldn't have been if she hadn't had such terrible taste in friends.

But I began picturing James spending that week

dripping poison into Nicole's ear about me. Then I cracked. I admit that.

'I'm sorry,' I cried. 'Him going on holiday with you is not appropriate, now you've got a boyfriend.'

Nicole laughed.

'It's not funny, either,' I said.

'Oh, yes it is . . . Come on, James is just a friend.'

'Are you sure he knows that?'

'Now you're being silly.'

'I don't want him going on holiday with you.'

A new note came into her voice. 'Danny, you don't run my life.'

I hesitated for a moment. I knew I should stop there. And I nearly did. But then Nicole said. 'And poor old James has been really looking forward to this holiday – he told me so today.'

Then it was as if a wave of blackness came over me – that's the only way I can describe it – and I whispered, 'If he goes on holiday with you, we're finished.' The words rushed out. I was just saying it because I was upset – and wanted to look big.

But Nicole cried out, 'How can you be so completely stupid?' and dashed out of Pizza Paradiso.

That was nearly a week ago.

We haven't spoken since. Oh, I've tried to talk to her so many times. I even sent her a card and letter with a two-page apology but all I've had in reply is one curt text message asking me not to contact her again.

I just can't believe she's dumping me because of one

stupid argument about James. Surely she knows she means the world to me and that's why I didn't want my deadliest enemy spending a whole week with her? Ask any boy – they'd feel exactly the same.

Well, Gary, for one, agrees with me. When I told him what had happened he patted me on the shoulder. 'Aaah, unlucky, mate . . . No, I can see you're really stoked and if I had a heart I'd be crying. But look on the bright side.'

'Which is?'

'You're single again.'

But I don't want to be single again.

If I could just see Nicole one more time, I know I could clear all this up. First, I'd admit that I'd made mistakes and tell her she could go on ten holidays with James if she wanted. Then I'd explain that my trouble is I want everything to be great between us all the time, and when it's not I get very frustrated. But now I promise I will listen to everything she has to say.

This is pretty much what I shouted at her through the traffic cone tonight. 'Give me one more chance and I won't let you down!' I yelled. 'And the improvement in me will be very dramatic!'

She must have heard all that. So why didn't she come outside? Would it have killed her to do that? Apparently it would.

But I'm not giving up yet.

I shall get Nicole back.

Chapter 7

THURSDAY 30 JULY

What a night!

It started with me trying to see Nicole again. I went along to the next Teens Take Action meeting but the way was barred by two girls and my dear old mate, James. It was good seeing his miserable, unsmiling face again – and how thoughtful of Nicole to have a little reception committee waiting for me.

One of the girls said to me, 'If you go in there, Nicole will only have to leave.' Actually, I knew she wouldn't see me, but what did I care about anything now? Something inside me had gone bitter. And right now I just wanted trouble.

James seemed in the mood for a fight, too. He twisted his face as he yelled, 'Just leave her alone,' and in such a patronizing tone. I immediately sent my fist flying in his direction. Well, he was asking for it. I wasn't going to stop there either, even though these girls were screaming at me to do just that. Who knows what would have happened if a voice hadn't called out, 'Come on, you're better than this.'

And there was a boy I'd never seen in my life before, yet grinning at me as if we were old friends meeting in a street full of strangers. I was so astonished by this; I even let him pull me off James. Then James started mouthing off, but the boy raised a hand and said, 'It's all over now. I'll look after him. You go into your meeting.'

James was led away by two girls. I stood there panting for a few seconds, staring at this boy. He looked about eighteen, maybe a bit older.

'Fights really are best avoided,' he said lightly.

I gazed up at him, confused. 'Look, I don't get what you're doing here.'

'Well, I knew this was a flashpoint and things might kick off here tonight.'

'You knew?' I repeated incredulously. 'So you're from the police?'

'Behave. I'll tell you who I am over a pot of tea.'

I gaped at this stranger, who'd strolled so confidently into my life. 'You want to buy me a cup of tea?'

'Yes, please.'

'And where will we go for this tea?' I asked suspiciously.

'A café in the town – little jewel of a place – very friendly. You'll like it.' He peered at his watch. 'But I've got another appointment in forty-five minutes so I'm going to have to rush you, I'm afraid. Are you coming or not?'

I felt a bit as if I were running away from a battle: broken and defeated. But, as I said to him, I really didn't have anything better to do.

And I'd never met anyone who walked as fast as him. Right at the top of the high street near the church was a place I'd hadn't been to before called the Copper Kettle. It was quite small and practically empty. Scattered over the walls were all these paintings of the countryside.

'Every one an original,' said the boy, noticing me looking at them.

Right at the back of the café was a little raised platform, like a small stage, and two tables with large, red-backed chairs. At one of the tables sat an old man – he looked like a little, withered nut – eating noisily. The other table had a RESERVED sign across it. The boy moved this and motioned me to sit down.

I felt suddenly very self-conscious. 'Never been in here before,' I mumbled.

'It's the best,' he replied.

I looked across to see if he was being funny, but I really don't think he was. The old man at the next table seemed to be having great trouble chewing his bun. 'If his teeth come out, I'm leaving,' I announced.

The boy gave a huge, cheeky grin. Then he leaned right back in his chair, arms spread behind his back, clearly very at ease here. He was wearing a black, pin-striped suit, a very loose black tie, which was halfway down his chest, and white trainers. He looked eccentric and arty. I asked, 'So what's this – adopt-a-hoodie week?'

He grinned. 'I really like you . . . you're great.'

I still looked at him suspiciously. There had to be a cruel punch line to all this. 'Is this some kind of joke, then?'

He leaned forward. 'This is certainly no joke, Danny.' He said this so seriously it took me by complete surprise. It was like a sudden burst of lightning.

'How do you know my name?' I demanded.

Before he could reply, this woman with very bright red hair appeared. She smiled warmly at the boy. 'Another busy evening, love?'

'Emergencies all over the place, Kathleen,' he replied. 'I put it down to the hot weather.' That intense seriousness had vanished now and there was relaxed good humour around him again.

'I know what you'll have,' she said fondly to him. 'But what about you, dear?' she asked me.

'I'll have tea as well,' I murmured.

She nodded, and then added in a friendly way, 'You're in good hands now.'

As soon as she'd gone I demanded, 'So come on, what's going on? And how do you know my name?'

'Oh, I know a lot more about you than your name,' he replied, gleefully. 'One of our investigators happens to live near Nicole.'

'One of your investigators?' I repeated incredulously.

'That's right, amazing people . . . I'd be lost without them.'

'But who exactly are they?' I persisted.

'It's best you know the bare minimum about them; that's not your business. The important thing is they've told me all about you and Nicole – although I'd like to know more.'

55

Then he smiled, as the woman with the red hair appeared with a tray containing two pots of tea.

'You get your tea here as it should be served – in a teapot. None of this teabag-in-your-cup lark, eh, Kathleen? As for the scones here: home-made and always warm from the oven – perfect.'

They laughed and chatted for a moment. After she'd left, he said he wanted to know some more about Nicole and me. You might wonder why I didn't just tell him to mind his own business. I've been puzzling about that, too. Maybe it was the way his eyes sparked with such total attention every time I spoke. It was kind of flattering, I suppose.

So I told him how at first Nicole and I had got on really well. In fact, whenever she felt a bit depressed (which she did surprisingly often) she said I was the only person who could cheer her up.

I went on to tell Rupert about the day Nicole visited my house. I'd dreaded her seeing my awful dump of a road, where all the houses look as if they've been thrown together and might blow away at any moment and there's always litter everywhere (I even cleaned all that up before Nicole came, as if she was royalty visiting us). But my mum and dad and even my two little brothers, for goodness' sake, made her so welcome – it was totally different when I called on her folks.

I suspected James might have put in some bad words for me (he, of course, was their favourite person in the entire universe). Anyway, they were both so stiff and cold that afterwards I told Nicole her parents were a pair of snobs.

She got mad and said I didn't know them . . . and soon we were having our first big row.

I took him through all the other rows, ending, of course, with that little beauty at Pizza Paradiso. And when I'd finished he leaned forward and said, 'Now, it's time I told you something about me.'

He began to speak very quickly. 'My name is Rupert but don't hold that against me. I run a small, secret organization. It's for teenagers only – although we have a couple of honorary, older members. Here's my card.'

He handed me a small card on which was just written 'The Ex-Files', and a phone number.

I stared at it. 'I still don't get what you do.'

'We stop people like you who've been dumped from making any more mistakes and we give you all the help you need.'

'But why would you want to help me . . .? You don't know me.'

'Because I was in your situation once,' he replied. 'I made every mistake you've ever made – and many more.'

It was hard to imagine this laid-back person ever charging about like a loon, as I'd been doing over Nicole. But there was a web of lines about his mouth and eyes, which made his face look unexpectedly sad when he wasn't joking.

He continued, 'I needed someone to put me straight but there wasn't anyone. I don't think that's right. So I set up a new organization to assist fellow sufferers.'

I thought for a moment. 'Do I have to pay for this?'

'Everyone always asks me about money,' he cried. 'No,

you won't have to pay a penny. Sometimes at the end of the cure people give us a contribution towards our running costs but it's up to you. You'll have to sign a contract, though. We do insist on that.'

'So, are you some kind of sect . . . for needy losers?' I added under my breath.

He grinned. 'A sect of dumpees. Well, it would be a pretty big sect, with millions of members.' He took a swig of tea, with obvious relish.

'But you'll help me get Nicole back?'

He shook his head. 'This is definitely not a dating service . . . In fact, really it's exactly the opposite. Our job is to help you put a relationship behind you . . . which, believe me, can be one of the hardest things in the world.'

He was talking quickly again now, and with such intensity, it was hard not to be swept along with him. 'When you're dumped so many emotions hit you – guilt, anger and a really terrible despair. This is a time when you need attention and support . . . especially when you're a teenager, going through it for the very first time. Yet not one single person seems to understand or be able to help. You're totally alone –'

'Until now,' I interrupted, 'with the Ex-Files riding to your rescue.' My tone was a shade mocking but actually I was becoming more and more intrigued by this whole set-up.

I asked some more questions, and then I went to the loo, really to think about this some more. While there, I glanced at my face. It had a weary, exhausted look which I'd never seen there before. So that's what you've done to me, Nicole. You've turned me into someone I hardly recognize.

When I got back Rupert said, 'I see my next appointment is plucking up courage to come in. I don't want to rush you, Danny. So why don't you go away and think about all this and let me know tomorrow, maybe –'

'I don't need to do that.' I interrupted so firmly, I shocked myself. But this guy seemed to know what he was talking about. And what did I have to lose? It was free – and I could do a runner at any time. 'I've decided I want to join up right now,' I said. 'So what happens next?'

'Tomorrow we meet up to sign the contract and debrief, either here or at your house.'

'At my house. All my family are out tomorrow . . . I suppose I'd better give you my address.'

'It's all right,' he replied. 'We have it already.'

A shiver ran down my spine. They really did know everything about me.

'See you tomorrow afternoon, then,' he said, 'at about two o'clock.'

As I left I saw that red-haired woman take Rupert up another cup of tea. For him, this little café must be like his office – but what a truly bizarre place to pick. It was like discovering MI5 operating from an old people's home.

The girl hovering about outside looked familiar. I was sure she went to the school down the road. I'd like to have spoken to her, only she had her head lowered as if she were in a spy film.

I watched her go inside: Rupert's next client. Or victim.

No, not victim. Too harsh. After all, he was helping people, wasn't he? Yet that makes you suspicious, for a start. I still don't understand why he should want to do that. This could just be an elaborate trick of some kind. Maybe you do end up paying him some money. And what about this contract he kept mentioning – perhaps there's a secret clause you don't read until it's too late.

What have I got myself into?

PART TWO

Taking the Cure

BELLA

Chapter 8

THURSDAY 30 JULY

I saw Rupert again tonight. Last night we just sat chatting in the bus shelter, but tonight we met up in a café called the Copper Kettle.

I was so surprised he'd picked that one. It was a really olde-worlde kind of place. You wouldn't have been surprised to see Miss Marple dropping in for a gossip.

When I first arrived I saw Rupert sitting right at the back of the café, deep in conversation with a good-looking boy I'm sure I recognized. This completely flustered me. I slunk out of the café again and hung about until the boy emerged. I quickly turned my face away. I didn't want him recognizing me and telling everyone what I was doing. And what exactly was I doing? I couldn't tell you. I'd tried to look on this encounter as a little adventure and kept telling myself I was seeing Rupert in a public place and could leave any time I wanted.

I edged back inside. Even at night, a sweet odour of

hot scones and chocolate still twisted itself round you. Rupert saw me and beckoned me over. His table had a large 'RESERVED' sign plastered across it.

'Turning into a busy night,' he said, conversationally.

The nerves got into my throat and I could only choke something in reply. Last night I'd talked away to him for ages about Luc and what had happened. It was like some kind of release, I suppose. And he was a surprisingly good listener – boys aren't usually, are they? But he seemed absolutely fascinated by everything I had to say. Afterwards, though, I feared I'd told him – a total stranger – too much. And why was he so interested, anyway? I even wondered if he was a reporter. But what newspaper would be running a story about me?

'What would you like to drink?' he asked me.

'Nothing,' I replied. 'Can't stay long,' I added. Meeting this highly inquisitive boy again was complete madness, not an adventure at all. I shifted about in my chair, which kept creaking. Then my nose started to run. I fumbled about for a hankie. He was looking straight at me now. His eyes were such a light blue; they were almost clear and quite impenetrable.

'You're wondering what you're doing here,' he said quietly. 'Shall I tell you?'

I nodded slowly.

'You're here because you can't believe how miserable you feel. In fact, right now it's crushing you. And you don't know how you're going to get through it.'

He was spot on there. But I didn't say anything.

'It's as if you're stuck in a dark, horrible place you've never been in before. Well, I've been to that place, too. And I know exactly how to get out of there . . . Interested?'

I hesitated. 'First of all, tell me what exactly you are.'

That question hadn't come out right at all. In fact, it sounded a bit rude, but he didn't take offence. Indeed, he seemed faintly amused. 'I'll tell you exactly what I am. I run a unique organization called the Ex-Files that's designed to help people who find themselves in your situation.'

'But why should you bother?'

'I'm always being asked that,' he replied, a trifle sadly. Then he said quickly, 'I bother because the Ex-Files is completely and totally brilliant.'

'Nothing like modesty.' I grinned. He was just about the strangest boy I'd ever met. He wasn't even a boy, really. I bet he was about nineteen or twenty; exuberant, yet with a strange authority about him and clearly very enthusiastic about what he was doing, whatever that was.

'Do I have to pay anything?' I asked.

He let out a thin sigh. 'Everyone always asks me that, too. The Ex-Files is free to all who use it . . . And, by the way, we guarantee complete confidentiality to all our clients, but we do ask in return that you say nothing to your friends and family about the Ex-Files. We can achieve so much more, undercover.' He couldn't hide that little smile of relish as he said 'undercover', either. I thought, *You're just loving the mysteriousness of all this*.

I said, 'So if I decide to join the Ex-Files, what happens next?'

'We either meet here or at your home.'

'Here,' I said at once, and then added, 'My dad's around tomorrow.'

'Good point,' he agreed at once. 'We prefer not to involve family members . . . So then, tomorrow you'll sign a contract.'

'Saying what?' I asked at once.

'That you'll sign all your money over to me for the next fifty years . . . No, that's a joke. It'll just say that you agree to abide by our rules. Then I will give you your first assignment – and the cure commences.'

'The cure,' I said. 'I like the sound of that.' And I suddenly noticed one of my feet was actually tapping.

I've arranged to meet Rupert again at eleven o'clock tomorrow. These past few days I've done so many things which have surprised me – cutting up dresses and stalking being just two of the highlights – so joining a secret society for dumpees fits perfectly into my bizarre new lifestyle.

I wonder what Luc would think if he knew what I was doing. He'd probably just be relieved I wasn't bothering him any more. I suppose the truth is I'm feeling very lonely right now – and Rupert is a great salesman. The trouble is, I'm still not exactly sure what he's sold me.

FRIDAY 31 JULY

I got a shock when I arrived at the Copper Kettle this morning. There was someone with Rupert. A girl of about his age: spiky, blonde hair and smartly dressed. She just looked so drop-dead cool I immediately felt intimidated.

Then came another shock. She was introduced to me as Juliette, the co-founder of the Ex-Files. I'd just assumed Rupert was in sole charge. You'd think having a girl involved as well would have reassured me, but oddly enough it didn't. She was too brisk and efficient for my taste; her presence seemed to take away some of the friendly relaxed atmosphere of yesterday. I also wondered if she was Rupert's girlfriend. That idea didn't exactly please me either – though don't ask me why.

Rupert was his usual, quirky self, though. 'Here's the contract. Read it, sign it, then you're in our power forever . . .'

I quickly read it. It said:

THE EX-FILES' CONTRACT

I promise to follow all the tasks decreed by **The Ex-Files**. I will take seriously all their advice. I will not discuss this agreement with anyone. In return, the Ex-Files promises not to disclose anything I have told them.

Please note the following **PENALTY CLAUSE**.

If you do not follow our advice, that's the last time you will ever see us.

Juliette must have noticed me raising my eyebrows at that part because she said, 'In the early days some of our clients let us down and misused the Ex-Files. And we do only have limited resources, so if you're half-hearted you're just wasting our time, aren't you?'

Now she was making it all sound like a business. I didn't like that – or her – very much, so I didn't say anything. Then Rupert cut in with a mocking grin, 'We can't just help anyone, you know. We have certain standards to keep up.' He laughed and I laughed too. He added, almost shyly, 'So pleased you've joined us.'

The last part of the contract just stated that the agreement took place on Friday 31 July between Bella Norris and the co-founders of the Ex-Files.

I signed it, and handed it to Rupert. He cried, 'Great. That's all the boring paperwork out of the way. Now we can move on to your first assignment.' He looked at me. 'People sometimes gasp when I tell them what it is.'

'I'm getting nervous now,' I said.

'I'm not surprised,' said Juliette, in her slightly drawly voice, 'after that build up.'

'Bella, for your first task,' cried Rupert, 'we want you to go straight home and scoop up everything that reminds you of Luc: cards, presents, photographs and letters. We want it all. We don't want a particle of Luc left in your house.'

'We'll provide you with a bag,' added Juliette, 'so you just shove it all in there and then give the bag to us.'

I hadn't expected that at all, and it seemed such a huge thing to ask. Right now all I had left of Luc were his cards and presents . . . and notes. There were masses of those. Often he'd slip a little note into my pocket, just saying how much he loved me. Later I'd find it and keep it in the little drawer by my bed, with all his other messages.

So if they were all taken away, that would leave me with nothing of Luc at all.

I sat thinking about this, while neither Rupert nor Juliette said a word. They just let the silence stretch out . . .

Suddenly the rest of the café seemed very noisy. It was as if someone had just switched the volume right up. I gazed around. No one, apart from us, was under forty in here and most were considerably older than that.

Two white-haired ladies on the table opposite were shaking with high-pitched giggles, while a man with a bushy beard was standing right in front of the fan, which was whirring away beside our table. 'It's just too hot,' he muttered to no one in particular.

What a very odd place for the Ex-Files to meet, but rather a clever one too. No chance of any teenagers overhearing what you were saying – they'd never be seen dead in here. You were totally and completely private! And the lady who served us – she's called Kathleen and has very bright red hair – was lovely. She kept smiling at me and said to let her know if I wanted anything else. I really felt as if I was getting special attention.

Minutes must have ticked by, but neither Juliette nor Rupert made any attempt to rush me. Perhaps they were used to this. Did most new members balk at doing something so dramatic for their first assignment? At last, I said quietly, 'Is it totally necessary?'

'I'm afraid it is,' replied Rupert. 'Hanging on to all that stuff just keeps the wound open . . .'

'And imprisons you in the past,' added Juliette.

'But what will you do with it?' I asked.

'We'll keep it very safe for you,' said Juliette. 'And one day, if you want it all back, it will be here, waiting for you –'

'As good as new,' cut in Rupert.

'But if you'd rather never see it again,' said Juliette, 'we'll also destroy it for you.'

I couldn't see that happening. And I still had my doubts. But then I glanced down at the penalty clause. I didn't want to be chucked out of the Ex-Files on my very first day. Besides, I could always keep back a couple of Luc's cards. They'd never know.

'All right,' I said slowly. 'I'll do it.'

As Dad would have left to have lunch with Gloria now I decided to do the deed right away. Rupert drove us back to my house in this ancient Rover, which he told me he'd borrowed from his grandad. Actually, I could have believed it was Rupert's: it would be just like him to drive such an eccentric choice of car.

At my house Juliette handed me a large canvas bag and said they'd wait for me. But I, of course, invited them inside. 'Make yourselves at home,' I said.

'We will . . . while you get to work,' said Rupert, tapping my bag. 'Nine out of ten relapses happen in the bedroom, you know. It's where you're at your most vulnerable: a real danger zone. So by removing everything that reminds you of him, you could say you're sterilizing your room and making it safe for you to go in.' I had a feeling he'd delivered this little speech many times before, but he said it with great conviction.

'Now, do you want any help?' asked Juliette gravely. She made it seem as if I were off to defuse a bomb.

'No, I'll be OK,' I said.

And actually, it wasn't anywhere near as hard as I expected. Seeing all Luc's little cards and presents didn't make me go all gooey and sentimental. Instead, they sent me into a blazing rage. He'd gone and dumped me, so what was the point of keeping all this junk? It didn't serve any purpose any longer, save to drag me back to a long, dead past.

So I positively flung the bracelet Luc had given me into the bag, followed by that massive birthday card and the six postcards he'd sent me when he was on holiday at Easter. Then I scooped up all his little messages which I'd so lovingly hoarded and hurled them into obscurity, too. At last I felt I was getting my own back on Luc.

I suddenly thought of Miss Haversham in that book we're reading at school: *Great Expectations* by Charles Dickens. Years and years after she'd been jilted at the altar, she still wore her wedding dress, was still waiting for her suitor to return. She'd even kept the wedding cake, now covered in cobwebs, of course. Shame they didn't have the Ex-Files in her day.

She was like a really dramatic illustration of what happened if you didn't move on: you just became a pathetic freak, so lost in past dreams you weren't really alive at all.

But just when I was feeling so strong and clear-headed and triumphant, I was ambushed by something I'd totally forgotten about. Right in the back of my bedside drawer were four snaps of Luc and me together in a photo booth. We were both fooling about, pulling stupid faces – nothing in the least romantic about those poses. And yet, I could catch the happiness in those silly snaps so strongly, it actually made me gasp, as if I'd just touched something very hot.

All at once I realized I'd just been pretending: I didn't want to make a fresh start at all. Inside that photograph was the only place I wanted to live. In fact, I just wished for one thing in the entire world: to go back to those days. There had to be a way back . . .

I looked up at my mum's photograph above the bed. Usually this calms me, makes me feel in some mystical way she's still here watching over me. But today it just added to my feeling of sadness, people being lost to me forever. A great wrenching pain shot through me, and hot, frustrated tears started rushing down my face . . .

'How are you getting on?' Juliette was standing in the doorway.

'Oh, I've got rid of most of them,' I said, hastily brushing my tears away. 'No, I'm doing fine,' I added, hoping she'd just go away. I knew she meant well but there was something very intimidating about her.

But she didn't go away; instead she sat next to me on the bed. She didn't say a word, though, so in the end I burst out, 'Well, as you can see, I am in fact having a bit of a relapse.'

'Oh, you'll have tons more of those,' she replied briskly.

'It was just seeing these really, daft photos . . . caught me unawares.'

'Shall I put them away?' she asked.

'No, I'll do it,' I said firmly. And I watched them flutter down into the bag. 'There, they've gone,' I said, as lightly as I could manage.

'Is there anything else?' asked Juliette.

'No, I think my room is fumigated from all memories of . . . Oh, I've forgotten his name already.' I gave an uncertain laugh.

'What about your ring?' asked Juliette. 'Did Luc give that to you?'

'He did,' I said softly. 'On Valentine's Day . . . So you want that too?'

'We'd much rather you removed it,' said Juliette. 'But we needn't take it away today. You can keep it here in a drawer or a cupboard, and then tomorrow . . .'

'No, have it now,' I said, slipping the ring off my finger. As I did so a shudder ran through me. Now I really was exorcizing Luc from my life.

'Nothing of him left here now,' I said, throwing the ring down into the bag.

Juliette brought out a tiny key from her pocket. Then she locked the padlock on the bag. 'Don't forget, you can have access whenever you want,' she announced.

'Thanks,' I replied. Then I asked, 'So have you and Rupert been doing this Ex-Files work very long?'

'No, not really,' she replied. 'About a year and a half

ago Rupert got dumped, really went through it. In fact, he said there are some months he can't remember at all . . . it's gone into total blackout.'

Rupert always seemed so cheerful and confident, but yet I could believe he'd had his heart badly broken. Just occasionally when he's talking about relationships, his smile will look sort of sad and tired, as if even now the memories can still snare him.

'Then it was my turn to get dumped,' said Juliette calmly. 'My boyfriend was a lot older than me and when he finished with me I wasn't talking to either of my parents so I was totally lost . . . until Rupert, who lived in the same road as me, took me under his wing.' A soft smile appeared fleetingly. 'He gave me all the advice we're giving you now and it totally turned my life around. We started helping other people we knew and then Rupert thought maybe other victims could benefit as well. So we set up our investigators – who are mainly people we've helped before – to be our eyes and ears, and tell us about deserving cases.'

'And someone told you about me?'

'That's right,' said Juliette. 'We've been watching over you for several days now.'

It was so strange to think of all this going on, totally unknown to me.

Then Juliette asked me, 'So are you all finished?' just as if I'd been to the dentist or something.

'Yes, all finished,' I replied.

Downstairs, Rupert gave me my second assignment.

'And this is probably the most important one of all – and definitely the toughest. You must never, ever ring Luc or email or text him or post him a letter or send him a smoke signal. And there are to be no more return visits to that bus stop.' He smiled a little. 'Or attempts to bump into him accidentally on purpose.'

'The important thing now,' added Juliette, 'is to hang right back and give him plenty of space.'

'All right,' I nodded.

Immediately Juliette and Rupert both grinned as if I'd just made a joke.

'You say that so easily,' smiled Rupert. 'But I promise there'll be times when you have such an intense craving to ring him or see him . . . The very second that happens, call us.' His tone had become so urgent I felt a bit alarmed. 'We mean that, Bella. Whatever time of day or night it happens, call us. Right?'

I nodded solemnly.

'And remember,' said Juliette, 'right now, you can't do a single thing to make him come back to you. You can only do things to make him not want to come back.' A look of understanding flashed into her eyes. 'Playing the waiting game really is the hardest bit of all.'

As they left, Juliette also gave me a card with her mobile number on, in case I'd rather chat with her than Rupert (I doubted this very much, although I liked her more than I did at first), and Rupert handed me an Ex-Files' Things Not to Do list.

THINGS NOT TO DO

- Never phone, text or make any contact with your ex!
- Never take any action regarding your ex without consulting your mentor first.
- Never compare yourself with your ex's new boyfriend or girlfriend. It will only depress you.
- Never slag off your ex in public. This just cheapens you.
- Never show how upset you are. Keep up a good front at all times.
- Remember:

THERE'S NO ONE YOU CAN'T GET OVER.

Chapter 9

WEDNESDAY 5 AUGUST

Gloria's just swooped in with Dad for a few minutes. She greeted me with the words, 'Oh, marvellous. You've lost all those terrible dark circles under your eyes. I've been so worried about you.'

Somehow I managed not to laugh out loud at that last remark. I do feel better, though. I'm sleeping in until at least six o'clock now (I'd been waking up every morning at around four o'clock) and, as I just said to Rupert on the phone, 'I've had a few little cravings for Luc but nothing major.'

Rupert congratulated me, then asked how I was getting on with my third assignment. This was to write down five things I like about myself. It seemed such a strange thing to do at first, but Rupert said being dumped can be a real confidence killer. This was to remind me what a great person I am.

Not only did I have to write out that list, I had to look at it first thing every morning.

'And are you doing that?' he asked. He sounded like a doctor checking I'd been taking my tablets.

'Yes, heaven help me, I am,' I laughed.

'Well, don't stop now, and if you ever want to add to that list . . .'

'Oh no, finding five things was really stretching it,' I said.

THURSDAY 6 AUGUST
2.30 p.m.

Now I've got another assignment (they certainly come thick and fast). This time I have to do three things I've never done before. And at least one of the three should be something that feels a bit daring. Rupert told me about one Ex-Files member who took up hang-gliding. As I gasped a bit at this he went on, 'But other members have started a new hobby or sport or given themselves a completely different look. It's entirely up to you.'

'And that's my homework for today, is it?' I said, just a trifle wearily. But still, I suppose these assignments do get you thinking about something else other than you know who.

3.30 p.m.

For one of my assignments I've decided I shall give myself a new look, starting with a completely different hairstyle tomorrow.

FRIDAY 7 AUGUST
11.35 a.m.

An emergency. Right out of the blue, as well.

At half past nine I had my hair cut. It's much shorter now, a bit like Juliette's, actually. I watched all my hair falling on to the floor; it was as if I was shedding my old self as well. The new me shimmered into my head: much more sophisticated and worldly and at ease with herself, not always trying to please other people either. Already I felt transformed.

Then, as I waited for my change, I stared out of the window. The early morning sun had been smothered beneath a heavy mist, but now that had thinned out and another, bright shiny day stretched out in front of me. I was determined to enjoy every second of it, too.

And then I saw him.

I saw Luc walk right past the window. He had his head down so he didn't notice me. But I spotted him all right.

Just a few weeks ago if I'd seen Luc I'd have belted out of that hairdresser's, his face would have lit up with joy upon seeing me and we'd have gone off somewhere together. But today if I raced up to him there wouldn't be the trace of a smile. There's nothing left between us now . . . except awkwardness.

An aching, desperate sadness crashed over me . . . and then I must have fainted. The next thing I knew I was sitting in a chair with my head between my knees. Embarrassing wasn't the word. The girl who'd cut my hair – a chatty girl, dressed entirely in black, called Jo – brought me a glass of water. Another woman who was waiting to have her hair permed loomed over me and asked if I'd eaten any breakfast.

It was ridiculous, really. I just glimpse Luc for a moment and I turn into this pitiful, shuddering thing. I was ashamed of myself. Still, I told myself, no harm done. And when I finally tottered out of the hairdresser's Luc, of course, had well and truly vanished. So the danger was over. Only it wasn't. In fact, it was only just beginning.

You see, when I saw Luc he was walking with his head right down looking so fed-up and dejected. Did that mean – was there just the tiniest chance? – he might be missing me?

The idea slipped away but then returned with re-inforcements! What if Luc is desperate to see me again but lacks the nerve to ring me up? That would be just like him.

I laughed out loud at myself, dreaming again.

Still, his walk was not a happy one. That was a fact. Something was bothering him. And it might be me.

Mightn't it?

MIGHTN'T IT?

Then, back in my bedroom I noticed something of Luc's which still lived in here – his CDs. I'd genuinely forgotten about them. Luc said I had lousy music taste (and I have) so he brought round his own CDs for us to listen to – and he'd never taken them back again. I expect he was missing them. And it would be quite a natural thing to call and casually enquire if he'd like them back.

Then Luc's got the chance to say . . . in my head I start imagining our conversation. But it's not real, I tell myself. I know that. The terrible thing about these cravings, though, is that they melt your mind.

And, quite suddenly, I found myself dialling Luc's number. I'll just very breezily ask him if he'd like his CDs back, that's all. His phone began ringing. Any moment now Luc could come on the line. But, all at once, it's not Luc's face which pops into my head, but Rupert's – gazing at me with such disappointment that I fling the phone away.

I just stand there panting for a few moments. Then I dial Rupert's number. He quickly grasps the urgency of the situation.

And he keeps talking to me, until he's got into his car. 'Now I'm about five miles away, so I just need you to be strong for a bit longer until I come round. Can you manage that?'

'I think so.'

'Well done! When I've rung off, put your mobile down immediately and go and sit in a different room – preferably one that hasn't got any phones in. Will you do that?'

'Yes, Rupert, I will.'

'I'll be there soon – if not sooner.'

So I'm waiting for him in the bathroom. The craving hasn't gone away at all. I still want to call Luc so badly. It's agony, actually.

But now I can hear a car.

I so hope it's Rupert.

1.30 p.m.

It was Rupert.

He made us both a cup of tea and then just let me talk.

'I almost spoke to Luc, you know . . . I dialled his number.'

'Happens to the best of us,' he said.

'It was just that he looked so miserable and –' my voice fell away – 'as if he were missing me.'

'Never, ever speculate,' said Rupert, 'because you're not thinking properly. You're just daydreaming.' He got up and looked out of the window. 'We've had Luc under unofficial surveillance, you know.' He sounded like a policeman.

'No, I didn't know,' I replied.

He turned round. 'It's all part of the service. We act as our clients' eyes, keeping a watch on their exs.'

'And what have you found out about Luc?' I asked.

Rupert shifted about for a moment. 'Early days, of course . . . but we know he went to a barbecue last night.'

I made a strange kind of choking noise, which was almost a laugh. 'So when I saw him he was just a bit hung over from the barbecue. He's been having the time of his life without me.' I laughed mirthlessly again.

Rupert sat down opposite me on the couch again. He spoke softly, urgently. 'Tell yourself you won't get back with Luc and your life will be so much better.'

I started with surprise. 'You mean give up all hope?'

'Well done, Bella,' he cried excitedly. 'You've grasped it right away. Hope is your biggest enemy . . . Hope keeps the fever bubbling inside you. Hope stops you from moving on.' He added grimly, 'And I'm an expert on this topic – I wrecked just about everything before I gave up hoping she'd come back to me.'

'But she never did?'

'Can you blame her? Night after night I used to stand outside her house. Spooky or what? I even started scaring myself. But I was totally off my head with hope. That's my excuse, anyhow.'

'How long exactly did all this last?'

'Oh, months and months, but I had no one to guide me. As a result, I failed all my A levels. In fact, I got unclassifieds, which is pretty tough to get. So I must have even misspelled my name.'

He laughed, shaking his head at the memory of it. 'But I didn't care about anything except her . . . So this last year, while my friends are at university, I've been to evening classes resitting all my A levels.' He leaned forward. 'Never feel embarrassed about telling me anything, Bella. Whatever mistakes you make, I've made far, far worse ones.'

'You've really cheered me up,' I said. Then we both laughed because that seemed a callous thing to say after hearing about his heartache. But I felt such a strong bond with him. He was the one person who knew exactly how I felt. And although all that stuff about giving up hope had shocked me at first, he was speaking from experience. And I could understand what he meant: when hope strikes it is like a fever, making you do the weirdest, most embarrassing things – well, hadn't I shown that today?

I wondered about the girl who'd so totally broken his heart. In fact, I would have loved to have found out some more about her, but I didn't want to seem nosy.

Rupert stayed with me until, as he put it, I was 'out of danger'.

'Absolutely no chance of me ringing Luc now,' I said.

He nodded approvingly.

'And I'm really, really pleased I didn't call him before. Think how humiliating that would have been. Thank you, Rupert, for saving me from that . . . Sometimes I think you're a bit like my guardian angel.'

I think Rupert really liked me saying that, because he grinned and said, 'Well, we all need one of those.'

D A N N Y

Chapter 10

MONDAY 10 AUGUST

Nicole's losing her power over me.

I've only been a member of the Ex-Files for a few days but already it's changed my life, exceeded all my expectations. It's a big deal, actually.

Their motto is: 'There's no one you can't get over.' And they say hope is our biggest enemy. I'm finding out how true that is. For instance, Nicole got back from holiday on Saturday and every time the phone went over the weekend hope boiled up inside me that it would be her. My head was thick with dreams of reconciliation – so did she call? Of course not. And I saw at first hand how destructive hope could be. And how hard it is to give up.

Mum and Dad noticed I was going through it this weekend. Mum even tried to talk to me about Nicole. I actually blushed. This wasn't a suitable subject for my mum even though . . . Well, I've never told anyone this, but my parents nearly broke up last year. Dad even moved out for a bit but then they went and saw some marriage guru or other and patched things up. Now I was quite impressed by that. I know Nicole and I were not married but I tell you, we didn't have the rows Mum and Dad had either. We just had a disagreement over James going on holiday – for which I have apologized.

I still can't believe she threw our whole relationship away for him! I only hope he's worth it. Maybe one day she'll meet a boy James will approve of – although personally, I have my doubts. I think the only guy James sees as Nicole's boyfriend is himself. But she'll have to find that out for herself because I don't care any more. Like I said, she's losing her power over me.

She's already vanished from my house. I had to give Juliette everything that reminded me of her. Considering we went out together for such a short time there was quite a haul. For a start, all those photos I took of her. Then there were other dead-stupid things like a ticket stub from our first-ever visit to the cinema and, would you believe, the itemized bill from Pizza Paradiso: all gone forever. I'm so excited because it also means my days as a 'weirdo wuss' (Gary's words) are nearly over.

No more glooming about. No more being in a permanently bad mood. No more lying awake every night, rehashing every single thing that has happened between us and feeling lousy, lousy, lousy.

Thanks to the Ex-Files I've taken a peek into a calmer, saner, totally Nicole-free world. I'm not completely there yet, but I'm well on my way.

THURSDAY 13 AUGUST
10.15 a.m.

I'm off to meet a girl later this morning. She's called Leah, she's fourteen and she supports the same football team as me (Chelsea) and . . . well, that's all I know about her, really. I've never met her in my life.

So yeah, it's a kind of blind date. Except it's not a date, it's meeting with a fellow-sufferer. Leah's also a member of the Ex-Files, one of its two youngest members, actually. (The other is me!!) She was dumped callously by her first serious boyfriend and it's taken her a long time to get over it, too.

It strikes me, the minute you go out with someone it's just like you're entering a war zone – and there's a strong chance you could eventually find yourself on the casualty list. Like poor Leah and me did.

Now Leah has said she'd like to chat informally with a boy, maybe have a few laughs with him too, just to get into the swing of things again. Juliette said the Ex-Files occasionally assign members a 'buddy' and she thinks Leah and I might be able to help each other. So we're meeting for lunch, 'totally informally' at Pizza Paradiso. Juliette said, 'I expect you'd rather old-timers like Rupert and me weren't there,' and I agreed Leah and me might chill out better on our own.

I told Gary about Leah, and he said it was about time I saw other girls. I also mentioned to him about the Ex-Files. I know I'm not supposed to tell anyone about that, but one thing about Gary – he's completely trustworthy. He'll never spill your secrets to anyone.

Anyway, he thought the Ex-Files was a total waste of

time. He didn't know why people couldn't just forget and move on. But then, the longest he's ever gone out with a girl is a week!

Still, he's coming with me to have a look at Leah. If she's anything like Juliette's description she'll be absolutely stunning. (Hope Juliette hasn't described me in too flattering tones.) I can't wait, actually.

I do still think about Nicole. And I still get flashbacks. Rupert said to expect that. But her days in my head are really numbered now.

In fact, this might be the last time ever I need to write about her. So have a nice life, Nicole, won't you? I know I will – maybe even with Leah. Who knows?

Chapter 11

**THURSDAY 13 AUGUST
3.30 p.m.**

When I was least expecting it, Nicole called me.

And just before I was due to meet Leah as well. I couldn't believe it when her number came up on my phone. Just seeing that knocked all the breath out of me, never mind hearing her say, 'Hello, Danny, how are you?' in her soft, silky voice.

'Oh, I'm great,' I gulped. 'Never better. Did you enjoy your holiday?'

'Oh yes,' she said a bit vaguely. Meanwhile, HOPE just exploded in my head. Sorry, Rupert, but I couldn't hold it back. Out of a clear, blue sky Nicole rings. What else was I to do but HOPE?

'Well, I'm glad you're OK,' she said.

'Very OK,' I replied, my heart hammering away.

Nicole paused for a moment, and then her voice grew even softer. 'The thing is, Danny, I thought I should tell you myself that I've just started seeing someone else.'

There was a silence as loud as an earthquake before I muttered, 'So what do you want from me, a reference?' and hope vanished as suddenly as it had erupted.

Then I said, 'Actually, I've just started seeing someone else too and was wondering if I should tell you.' And just so she didn't think I was making it up: 'Her name is Leah and she supports Chelsea and I'm just off to meet her now, actually, at Pizza Paradiso.'

Nicole wasn't expecting that at all. She never for a moment suspected I could move on as swiftly as her. 'Well, I'm really pleased for you,' she said in a dazed kind of voice.

'Yeah, and I hope you and James will be very happy . . . It is James you're seeing now?'

'Oh no,' she replied. 'It's a boy I met in Brighton. He's coming to stay with me for a while and I thought you might hear about us . . . and I'd rather you knew ahead of everyone else.'

'Oh yeah, it's great to be first with the news,' I said bitterly. 'Anyway, I'd better not keep Leah waiting, she gets so impatient for me.'

I didn't even wait for Nicole to reply. I just rang off. The next thing I knew my doorbell had rung four times and a voice was yelling, 'Come on, bring out your dead!!' It was Gary.

I told him what had happened. He said, 'But the great thing is, you weren't lying – you really have got this gorgeous new girl waiting for you.'

And when we reached Pizza Paradiso Leah was already there, sitting, as arranged, at the table just by the window.

And she was even more beautiful than Juliette had described, with a heart-shaped face and very big eyes. Gary let out a low whistle of appreciation and muttered, 'Go on, my son, get stuck in.'

Top advice – but I didn't follow it. Instead I said, in a low, defeated voice, 'It's no good, I can't go in there.'

'Hey, brain-donor,' cried Gary scornfully. 'Look at her.'

I nodded miserably. 'I know, but it's no good, my head's all over the place now. And I'd be terrible company.'

I thought Gary would explode with derision. 'If you let that stuck-up cow, Nicole, sabotage this, you're a total loser.'

I was in complete agreement, and then I asked Gary if he'd tell Leah I couldn't make it.

'So what exactly do I tell her?' he demanded.

'I don't know. Tell her I've got chickenpox. Tell her I've been unavoidably kidnapped. Tell her anything. Only be very gentle and give her my fullest apologies . . . and say I'll make it up to her!'

Gary scowled at me and shuffled inside the café. We've got the same colour hair and are about the same height, so Leah didn't look very surprised to see him. I waited for Gary to explain and for her to jump to her feet – which was my cue to scuttle away. Only that didn't happen.

Gary sat down opposite her. He's obviously breaking it to her gently, I thought. They chatted for what seemed like ages. She was smiling as well. And then he started ordering food.

I watched all this with growing bewilderment. What on

earth was going on? Finally, Gary got up but he didn't leave. Instead, he made for the loos and a few seconds later my mobile started ringing.

'You just go home and dream about Nicole,' said Gary. 'I'm taking over here.'

'You can't do that,' I cried indignantly.

'Well, it's better than the alternative, isn't it?' said Gary, not altogether unreasonably. 'The thing is, she thinks I'm you and I thought it would just seem too weird if I went into a long explanation. So I'm you, all right?'

'Oh yeah, steal my identity, why don't you?'

'I'm only borrowing it,' he said, 'to cheer up a poor, broken-hearted girl.'

'You fancy her, don't you?' I said.

'What guy wouldn't . . . Oh, sorry, you don't, do you? Well, I'd better not keep my date waiting any longer. Don't worry; I'll make sure you give her a really good time. Bye.'

I took one last look at them before I left, teeming with envy now. That should have been me sitting opposite that beautiful girl. Well, in a way it was me, of course.

Why exactly did Nicole ring me? Did she think she was being kind breaking the news gently to her ex, who she's moved on from so swiftly? (And they say it's boys who are tough and insensitive.) No doubt her brand-new boyfriend is . . . No, I don't even want to think about him. I just want to say if she hadn't rung and got me all stirred up again, I'd be having a great day now.

So she's messed up my life yet again.

5.35 p.m.

My new girlfriend has just rung to thank me for a great lunch. This didn't seem the right moment to inform her that we've never actually met.

Got the surprise of my life when she called. I'd totally forgotten we'd been given each other's mobile numbers. Luckily my voice isn't that different from Gary's – only his is probably a bit deeper. So when I growled, 'Hey, Leah, how are you?' I sounded just like Darth Vader. No wonder she asked me if I was all right. 'Getting a bit of a cold,' I explained and threw in a little cough to add atmosphere.

'Oh, I'm sorry.' She sounded genuinely concerned. 'Hope you're well for tomorrow.'

'Tomorrow,' I echoed uncertainly.

'We're still going bowling, aren't we?'

It was the first I knew of it. Gary really should have filled me in on vital facts such as these.

'It is still on?' she asked, with a definite little throb in her voice.

'Oh yeah, it really is,' I said hastily. 'Looking forward to it already.'

'Well, I just wanted to thank you for really cheering me up. I haven't laughed so much for ages. See you soon then, Danny.'

Immediately afterwards I rang Gary to find out more about my second get-together with Leah.

'We're just going bowling – it's no big deal.'

'Well, make sure you look after her properly,' I said. Gary has rather a bad reputation where girls are concerned.

'I'll give her the time of her life,' he replied, then he laughed. I didn't like the sound of that laugh. And all the time I was talking to Gary I had a bitter taste of jealousy in my mouth. It should be me out with Leah tomorrow.

THIS IS THE VERY LAST TIME NICOLE WILL STOP ME FROM ENJOYING MYSELF.

FRIDAY 14 AUGUST

I cooked up this plan. While out bowling with Leah tonight, Gary will confess he is an impostor. Next he will announce, 'Here's the real Danny,' and up pops me.

'Then what happens?' Gary asked, when I told him. 'Does Leah continue the evening with both of us or does she have to send one of us home . . . or maybe she'll just think we've both been having a big laugh at her expense?'

That was the very last thing I wanted, especially as I know she's in a very fragile state at the moment. And if it's Gary playing me that she likes, who is to say she will like the real Danny as much?

So I'm afraid Gary's right; we'll just have to wait a bit longer for him to reveal he isn't actually me. Dead frustrating, though.

Still, the fact that I'm interested in other girls – well, one girl, Leah – is proof I'm practically cured of Nicole.

Chapter 12

SATURDAY 15 AUGUST
11.30 a.m.

Something totally incredible has just happened.

My parents and my two little brothers left early this morning (well, at 9.30 a.m., and to me, that's early on a Saturday morning) for Alton Towers. I went back to bed and had actually drifted off to sleep again, when the doorbell rang about an hour later. I looked fuzzily out of my bedroom window. Someone was pacing about very impatiently in my drive. And it was the very last person I ever expected to see, even more unexpected than Nicole.

I blinked in disbelief at the figure glowering on my doorstep, then threw on some jeans and a T-shirt and tore downstairs. I opened the door just as it rang for a second time.

I was deathly quiet for a moment. Then fury rushed back as I realized that the person I hate more than anyone else on the planet was here on my doorstep. I practically yelled, 'You've got a nerve!'

James – for yes, it really was him – replied curtly, 'Believe me, I wouldn't have come here if it wasn't an emergency.'

A wisp of hope stirred inside me. He'd brought a message from Nicole. She wanted to come back to me.

But then he said, 'Nicole doesn't know I'm here.'

'So what's all this about?' I demanded.

'I'm very worried about her,' he said. 'And I'd rather not continue this conversation on the doorstep.' His jaw was clenched so tightly his voice seemed to be coming from somewhere else. He was hating every moment of this. So what had happened to Nicole to bring him round here? A shiver of apprehension ran through me.

'You can come in for a minute,' I said. We walked into the kitchen in grim silence. We could have been on our way to a funeral. I didn't offer him a drink. I didn't even invite him to sit down. We faced each other like two opponents before a duel. I was fighting this angry lump in my throat. It really was thanks to him Nicole and I had broken up, and I'll never forget that.

He moved nearer to me.

'Now, you're standing too close,' I said. 'And I hate it when my skin starts crawling.'

He edged back. 'I shan't take up very much of your time,' he said pompously. He twisted his face up and announced to the ceiling, 'Nicole's got a new boyfriend.'

'Old news,' I called out.

He ignored this and went on conversing with the ceiling, in his dry, little voice. 'He seems very friendly and likeable.'

I shifted about impatiently.

'So this new boyfriend completely fooled me, I admit that.' All at once he had my full attention. 'But now I can see that he's messing Nicole about, playing stupid games . . . I'm not happy about that relationship at all.'

'Well, so what!' I snapped. 'What's it got to do with you, anyway?'

'I have her best interests at heart –' he replied quietly.

'Says you . . .' I interrupted sneeringly.

He paused. There were little beads of sweat on his forehead. 'Personally, I think she deserves someone better than either of you.'

'Like you, I suppose.'

His eyes went narrow. 'She's never, ever looked at me in that way. She went out with this other guy on the rebound from you. I think she might still like you.'

'Oh, really.' I struggled to make my voice sound amused and unconcerned.

'If I can arrange it, would you be prepared to meet Nicole again?'

I looked at him incredulously. 'Why on earth would you do that?'

He swallowed. 'For Nicole . . .' he began, then stopped and just repeated, 'For Nicole.'

Only a few days ago I'd have jumped at such a deal . . . no questions asked. But now was different. I was getting back in the flow of things again. I even had a possible girlfriend . . . Well, she hasn't actually met me yet but that was just a minor technicality.

And the Ex-Files have done a really great job of curing

me of Nicole. Rupert said only yesterday what great progress I'm making. Do I really want to go back to how I was before – a miserable obsessive, whose head contained only her?

Most importantly, can I trust James? Maybe Nicole was actually quite happy with her new boyfriend, and James just wanted to mess things up for his own murky reasons.

'Of course, if you don't care about her any more.' James's words shot round my tiny kitchen.

Stung now, I exclaimed, 'Just who do you think you are, saying I can see Nicole again? Why is it up to you? Isn't it time you got a girlfriend of your own?'

'I shall leave now,' interrupted James stiffly.

He walked briskly to the front door. I growled at his back, 'Tell me exactly why you want me to meet up with Nicole?'

He turned. 'Because I think it might get her out of his clutches.' For some reason he was whispering now, 'And that's what would be best for Nicole.'

'You really could bear her to go back out with a Chav like me?'

'You're better than the alternative,' he hissed. 'Just.' He went on. 'I shall need you to call me with your decision later on today.'

'Only a twenty-four-hour offer, is it?'

He didn't answer and stalked away.

What exactly is he up to? The more I think about this, the more confused I get.

That's why I'm going to consult Rupert right now. He'll know what to do.

1.30 p.m.

I never thought I'd have an argument with Rupert . . . but I just have.

I rang him, and he was round here in a flash. There was a gleam in his eye as he exclaimed, 'James turning up at your house this morning, why, that's the shock of the century,' and we both laughed about it like two good mates. But when I suggested that I go along with what James suggested, he shook his head very firmly.

'Look, I'm really not expecting anything,' I explained. 'I'm just dead curious to know what James is up to.'

'No, you must leave that to us,' replied Rupert, firmly. 'I've got people working on it already. They'll smoke out the truth.'

Usually I really like the way Rupert acts as if he's the head of some worldwide organization. But just then I found it irritating. Why this big drama? Why couldn't I find out for myself what was going on?

Rupert smiled wryly. 'Look, I know how tempting James's offer is, but it must be resisted at all costs. Something is wrong here; I can feel it . . . and do not, under any circumstance, contact Nicole about this . . . that would be a really fatal error.' I thought, *He's really piling the pressure on me now*.

Now, I think Rupert – and Juliette – are great. I've got masses of respect for both of them. But just occasionally, I resent the way they – and especially Rupert – think they can completely take over my life. Advice is great, but don't give me orders. Don't tell me what to do. I really hate it when people do that.

Anyway, before I knew it, Rupert and I were doing battle – over James, of all people.

Rupert wanted me to call James immediately and say I had no interest in his scheme. I replied that I'd do it later.

'It's best if you do it now,' said Rupert.

'No, I'll do it later,' I said again.

Rupert's voice grew icicles. 'We'd greatly prefer it if you closed down things with James now.'

We'd greatly prefer . . . Now and again Rupert really gets up my nose, especially the way he thinks every situation in life can be dealt with by referring to one of his rules. Well, I just don't think that's true.

'I'll do it later,' I said, for the third time.

For one awful moment I thought Rupert was going to chuck me out of the Ex-Files for insubordination or something, but he just said, quietly, 'All right, we'll leave it there – for now.' I knew he was highly annoyed with me, though. Then he growled, 'Hold your nerve, Danny.'

'Don't you worry about me,' I growled back.

He left without another word – and I just feel more mixed up than ever now.

3.45 p.m.

Well, I've finally come to a decision about James's proposal. After Rupert left the rain roared down. And I was staring out at it, wondering if there was any truth at all in what James had said about Nicole and her new boyfriend, when the doorbell rang. It was Juliette. *Now it's her turn to turn the screws on me*, I thought. But she breezed in, shaking the rain off her hair and demanding a cup of coffee.

She very quickly stretched herself out on the sofa. She was like a very sleek, confident cat. Drop-dead cool. I'd have just loved her as an older sister.

I said to her, 'I suppose you think I should forget about what James said to me, too?'

She looked at me with her small, quick, clever eyes and purred, 'Not easy to do. But yes, I think you'd be better concentrating on Leah. I hear last night was lots of fun.' I felt my face burning with embarrassment. In all the drama today I'd forgotten all about that. And Gary hadn't called me with an update either.

'She told me,' went on Juliette in confiding tones, 'she hasn't laughed so much for ages, as she did last night. I just knew you two would get on.'

Very keen to change the subject, I asked, 'Tell me if I'm being nosy, but are you seeing anyone at the moment?'

'Yes, I am.' Her eyes crinkled at the corners. 'Want to know more?'

'I'd love to know more,' I replied.

'Well, I've been seeing him for about two months . . . A very nice guy, only I don't think he's someone who's the answer to everything. I'm more realistic these days. But yes, we're having fun.'

'Good for you,' I said. 'And what about Rupert? Is he?'

'No, he's not seeing anyone. Says he's just too busy at the moment.'

So he's using the Ex-Files to distract himself from his

lousy love life. That nasty thought just whizzed into my head. I felt disloyal for even thinking it.

'You and Rupert have never gone out together, then?' I asked.

'We're always being asked that – and no.' Then she added, 'But he's the only person I completely trust. By the way, I think he sees a lot of himself in you.'

'In me?' I exclaimed.

'Definitely. For a start, you're both dreamers.' She suddenly looked straight at me. 'He really doesn't want you to make the same mistakes as him.'

'And going along with James's plan – even out of sheer curiosity – would be an earth-shattering mistake, would it?' I asked, with undisguised sarcasm.

She said, quietly, 'Well, let's consider the facts. James hates your guts and played a role in breaking you and Nicole up –'

'A very big role,' I cut in.

'A new boyfriend turned up last night and the following morning James is round to you, saying this boyfriend is all wrong and he'll arrange for you and Nicole to reunite. I agree with Rupert, that doesn't feel right. I can't put my finger on what James is up to – but it could be he's so riddled with jealousy over the new boyfriend that he's bringing you back to provide some fireworks . . .' She paused significantly.

And that really was the most likely explanation. The least likely was that James was doing me a good turn. Martians will land on Earth before that's true.

And James claiming Nicole wanted me back was his bait. He knew I'd be in a high fever of excitement after that. Then he could sit back and watch me fall into his trap. And afterwards, when I discovered that James had used me for his own devious purposes . . . still more pain and humiliation for me. The whole experience would, no doubt, go on eating away at me for days afterwards.

I realized now why Rupert was so insistent about not calling James. He and Juliette wanted to save me from going back to feeling angry and miserable all the time. I was just too emotionally involved to see through James's ruse at first.

'That James must think I'm a right mug, falling for a plan like that,' I announced to Juliette. 'I'm going to call him right now.'

It was quite a brief conversation. I merely informed him I wasn't interested in what he had planned. He sounded surprised, even shocked. He'd expected me to fly back.

And if it hadn't been for the Ex-Files I'm certain I'd have done just that.

I'm going to leave any further investigations into James's plot to them. I also realize now there's no chance of Nicole and me ever getting back together. I sort of knew it before. But now I see the hopelessness of it all so clearly.

It's over forever.

PART THREE

Beware the Relapse

BELLA

Chapter 13

WEDNESDAY 19 AUGUST

It was a total surprise.

I thought I was just going to the Copper Kettle this evening to update Rupert on how I was doing. But when I arrived at the café there was a CLOSED sign on the door, which gave me a jolt. Then Kathleen opened the door and grinned at me. 'Thought we needed a bit of privacy tonight,' she said in a conspiratorial tone.

It was completely empty except for Rupert and a girl called Zoe, who's the year above me at school. Everyone knows her – she's always being sent out of assembly for laughing – bright-eyed, vivacious and something of a party animal. So it was quite a shock to find her sitting in the Copper Kettle, chatting with Rupert.

He beckoned me over.

'You know Zoe, don't you?' said Rupert. Without waiting for me to answer he went on, 'She's the one who put us on to your case.'

She said, 'I heard all about what Andrea was up to with your boyfriend when you were on holiday . . . What a rat-bag, eh?'

I nodded and smiled.

'I got so mad about it all, didn't I, Rupert?'

'Kept on and on about it,' he said. 'She said if anyone needed the support of the Ex-Files, it was you.'

I couldn't help blushing.

Then I said, 'So you must be one of these investigators Rupert's always telling us about?'

'I am indeed, but I like to fly below the radar so no one realizes I'm picking up all the news.'

And who would have thought lively, light-hearted Zoe had been leading this double life? It must be quite exciting really, spying for the Ex-Files. 'Well, thank you very much for recommending me,' I said to Zoe.

'No, no, it's at times like this you need the Ex-Files . . . I mean, that's what it's all about.'

'And Zoe's invited here today,' announced Rupert, 'because it's a special occasion.'

'Is it?' I asked. 'In what way?'

'You'll find out,' he said with a gleeful smile. 'And Kathleen's going to join us because she's in the Ex-Files, too . . . an honorary member.'

'A very ancient one,' said Kathleen, coming and sitting at Rupert's table. It was quite a squash now and I wondered what exactly was going to happen next.

'Got a few questions for you,' said Rupert.

'Question one: have you, at any time in the past two weeks, called Luc?'

'No,' I said at once.

'You get a massive tick for that.' And he ticked this form he had in front of him. 'Have you emailed, texted or written him a letter?'

'No, no, no,' I said. 'Do I get three ticks for that?'

'Now you're just getting greedy. In the last two weeks have you ever stood outside his house or hung about in the bus shelter (he flashed a quick smile at me after saying that) opposite Andrea's house?'

'I can truly say I haven't.'

'Doing very well,' he announced, ticking another box. 'Have you ever tried to meet him accidentally on purpose?'

I hesitated.

'Ah,' he cried.

'No, really, I haven't. I did see Andrea yesterday . . . but that really was totally unplanned. I just bumped into her.'

'Tell us exactly what happened,' said Rupert quietly and I could sense everyone moving in more tightly around me.

'I was in town, on my way back from my Pilates class and I saw Andrea coming towards me. I thought, *I shan't swerve away from her. I've done nothing wrong.*'

'Too right,' murmured Zoe.

'So I said, "Oh hi, Andrea," very confidently but with a little air of mystery too. She was very embarrassed – more than me, really. But she said she liked my new hairstyle and told me to call her sometime. Of course, hell will freeze over first (everyone laughed). And then I went off and felt this little glow of pride because I hadn't tried to find out anything about her and Luc.'

'Excellent,' said Rupert and there were murmurs of agreement. 'You have also successfully completed all your assignments, so it is my great pleasure to tell you that you have passed, totally successfully, Phase One of your course. We have a certificate, but also –' at this point Kathleen jumped up – 'we do have a cake which Kathleen has made in honour of this momentous occasion.'

She returned holding a chocolate cake, with one candle right in the middle.

'Now, how did you know I love chocolate?' I said. 'Don't tell me, Rupert, you've got someone investigating the favourite foods of all your clients?'

'That's it,' laughed Rupert. 'For weeks our investigators have been following you into all these sweet shops . . .'

In the middle of the cake-eating, Juliette arrived. She'd been out on an emergency and later she, Zoe and Rupert went into a bit of a huddle. Rupert called over to Kathleen, 'Show Bella all your paintings and tell her who did them all.'

Of course, I'd noticed the paintings of the mountains and beautiful countryside in the Copper Kettle before and I'd guessed Kathleen had painted them, even though she hadn't signed any of them, just put her initials right in the furthest corner.

But I didn't know the pictures were all of Killarney in southern Ireland, where Kathleen had grown up. She spoke with such affection of all the places she had painted, and then said, 'But I think my favourite painting is of the Blarney Stone . . . and you'll see where I've put that one.' She pointed. It was right above where Rupert sits. 'Now is that appropriate or what . . . that boy can talk, can't he?'

I agreed he could. 'I was one of the very first people he helped, you know,' said Kathleen.

Then, without any prompting, she started telling me how her husband of seventeen years had just walked out on her one day. 'He left me a little note by the bread bin,' she said. 'Wasn't that thoughtful of him? He said he'd met someone else now – and he was sorry about that . . .'

'How awful,' I said.

'It's what people do to each other,' she replied, in a dull, toneless voice. 'But I don't miss him one little bit now. Me and my mum –' I suddenly remembered an older, very smart looking lady I'd noticed putting out menus as reverently as if they were hymn sheets – 'are happy and snug here . . . and, of course, I meet all Rupert's . . . I was going to say patients but that's not what you are, is it?'

'Sometimes I feel as if I am,' I said, smiling.

She threw up her chin and declared, 'I'll tell you what we all are: a clan. The clan of the broken-hearted; how about that?'

Then she sped off to get us some complimentary tea and coffee and later everyone drank a toast to me. Yet I felt suddenly apprehensive. Did all this celebrating mean the Ex-Files had finished with me now? I really didn't want that to happen. 'So am I all cured, then?' I asked, dolefully.

For a moment no one spoke; they all just smiled rather sadly at each other. 'I'm afraid not, Bella,' said Rupert gently. 'In fact, one day, just when you're least expecting, it will strike . . .'

'What will?' I asked.

He frowned for a moment. 'We call it the "big relapse". And every single person has to go through it. It'll come right out of the blue as well. You might have had a whole week without even thinking about him . . . then, just when you drop your guard, wham!'

'So what starts it off?' I asked.

'We do have a detailed fact sheet on this topic,' he said.

'I thought you might,' I said, with a teasing smile. 'Just tell me what starts it off.'

Rupert considered for a moment. 'Well, the funniest little things can jog your memory and take you right back to your time with him.'

'Then you'll start going all soft on him again,' said Juliette.

'That's when you're in very grave danger,' went on Rupert, cheerfully. 'But don't worry, we'll see you through it.'

'And how long does the big relapse last?' I asked.

Rupert considered. 'Five or six days is about the average.'

'Oh, mine was much longer,' murmured Juliette.

'Show off,' smiled Rupert.

'Well, nice to have something to look forward to,' I said.

'It's not always that bad,' cried Zoe.

'Yes, it is,' said Rupert firmly. 'But the good news is,

once you've come through this stage your ex's power over you just seeps away. So look on it as another stage in your recovery . . . and we'll be with you every step of the way.'

THURSDAY 20 AUGUST

The sun woke me up early, slithering through the curtains. After a few days of winds and heavy rain the sunshine was back with a vengeance. In fact, it was so hot I gasped when I went outside, just as if I'd stepped into a scalding bath. I lay in the back garden listening to the radio, with Tilly snuggled up beside me.

Then I must have drifted off to sleep because I didn't hear the doorbell – neither did Tilly. I was woken up by Tilly growling softly, and peered up at a tall figure looming over me.

I gave a start and then heard a familiar voice say, 'Yeah, it's me again.'

My eyes seemed stuck together and for a moment I wondered if I was completely awake. I sat up, blinking. There was something dream-like about Rupert suddenly appearing like some sort of heavenly messenger in my garden.

'You didn't answer the door but I heard the radio so I decided to try the back,' he said. 'We felt your life would be so incomplete without this.'

I gazed blearily at the certificate he handed me. It said: CONGRATULATIONS, BELLA, YOU HAVE PASSED PHASE ONE. Then, in tiny letters at the bottom, was written: The Ex-Files.

He explained, 'We make it fairly enigmatic, just in case

113

it should fall into the wrong hands . . . but I thought you might like to keep it somewhere private.'

'Yes, I would, thank you.'

He bent down to pat Tilly, who was now dancing excitedly all around him. For once he wasn't in his suit. He was wearing black jeans and a very pale, blue shirt, which matched his eyes.

'Would you like a cup of tea?' I asked.

'No, I can't stop.' He gave a quick, little embarrassed smile. 'Just been up to the college to get my A-level results, actually.'

'Oh, how did you get on?'

'Passed them,' he said shortly.

'Hey, well done, and do you wish to reveal your grades?'

'Three As, actually,' he said shyly.

I grinned. 'Show-off. No, well done, you must be really chuffed.'

'Well, better late than never, I suppose. I'm just on my way back to tell my nan and grandad.'

I remembered Juliette saying how Rupert lived in a cottage with his grandparents: his mum was dead (and that made another little bond between us, I felt); his dad was still alive but worked mainly abroad and Rupert hardly saw him – though he regularly sent Rupert large cheques, apparently.

Funny how I prized every piece of information I could find out about Rupert. I'd store it all away and think about it afterwards. Something else Juliette had told me flashed into my head.

'So you'll be able to go to Birmingham University in October, then?'

'Looks like it,' he agreed.

And suddenly I blurted out, 'But what about the Ex-Files?' Immediately I thought what a selfish question to ask. And anyway, I wasn't especially bothered about the Ex-Files – it was just me I was really thinking about.

'Don't worry,' he said. 'When the time comes Juliette is ready to take full responsibility. She believes in the Ex-Files just as much as me.'

'Yes, right,' I agreed, feeling ashamed I'd even asked that at his moment of triumph.

After he left I followed him in my mind to his house. I pictured him there with his grandparents clustered round him, anxious to hear how he'd got on. They'd be so excited when they found out his results . . .

Then I started imagining another scene: the end of September when Rupert leaves for university. And I suddenly realized just how much I was going to miss him.

DANNY

Chapter 14

FRIDAY 21 AUGUST
3.00 p.m.

I blame Nicole for what's just happened.

If she hadn't rung me seconds before I was due to meet Leah . . . well, none of this mess would have started. And now events have taken a definite turn for the worse: Gary only wants to finish meeting up with Leah.

He says things are getting too intense. 'She keeps asking me about my feelings. He made a face. 'I'm the wolf of the pack . . . and I don't want to turn into a care bear. I'll leave that to you.'

He's supposed to be having a pizza with her this evening. I assumed he was going to break it to her then. But now he wants to cancel the meal and just send her an email saying he'd rather not meet up with her again for a while. He says it's kinder that way.

I went mad when he told me. And in the end I said I was taking over and that I'd break it to Leah myself. Only

I'd do it with a bit of tact and diplomacy. I feel I owe her that at least.

See what a mess Nicole has left me with?

8.30 p.m.

Just thinking about tonight brings me out in a cold sweat.

I didn't spot Nicole in Pizza Paradiso first of all. I was so intent on what I had to do.

Leah was sitting in exactly the same spot as when I'd first seen her. She was staring into space with a little smile on her face, quite unaware of what lay ahead of her.

I thought, *I've got to do this as gently and painlessly as possible.*

'Hello,' I said. 'I'm a mate of Danny's – Gary.'

'Oh hi,' she replied. 'Is everything all right?'

'Not exactly,' I began. 'You see, Danny has been un-avoidably detained.'

She immediately looked worried. 'Oh, has his grandad been taken ill?' she asked. 'I know he was worried about him.'

Gary's grandad – and his illnesses – was a creature of pure myth, used regularly to get Gary out of situations. I smiled grimly. And then, to my horror, I saw Nicole sitting at a corner table with her boyfriend. I stared at her, utterly dazed and dumbfounded. For a moment everything else just fell away. I glanced at her boyfriend. He was quite good-looking in an oily kind of way, I suppose. He was whispering some-thing to her and she was giggling away.

Then I had a bit of a flashback – only to be expected –

but the Ex-Files had trained me well. After a couple of deep breaths I returned to the health of Gary's grandad.

'I'm afraid he's in a very bad way,' I said to Leah.

She looked so upset, I added, 'Well, actually, he's only in a bit of a bad way, hardly anything at all really, but Danny felt he should be with him.'

Suddenly I noticed Nicole watching me. I promptly sat down opposite Leah and declared, 'But Danny said we were to go ahead and have a pizza on him.'

'Isn't that just like him?' she said. 'Danny's a great person, isn't he?'

'The very best,' I agreed.

So Leah and I chose our pizzas and chatted away. She was very easy to talk to, very easy to look at as well. I sensed Nicole darting a few more glances my way. That pleased me a lot. I wanted her to see that I had moved on and got myself a beautiful new girlfriend.

But now and again this haunted look came into Leah's eyes, which hinted at less happy times. I sensed that she'd been very badly hurt by her last boyfriend. I was absolutely determined she'd enjoy herself tonight. In fact, Leah and me were having such a top time I nearly forgot what I was doing there, and that I was, actually, the bearer of some news that would severely dent – if not smash – the party spirit. But I decided I couldn't tell Leah while she was tucking into her pizza. Let her at least enjoy her food first.

I even wondered if I should set up another meeting with her and force Gary to come along and do his own dirty work, only it is very hard to force Gary to do anything. So what about if I arranged to see her again and tell her then? But what was the point of that? I was merely prolonging this poor girl's misery. No, she had to be told tonight.

Anyway, I did have some good news for her, too: I was still available, of course. I'd have to meet her as Gary first of all, but a bit later I could reveal my true identity. I was thinking this all out frantically while she carried on eating.

Finally she declared she couldn't eat another thing. 'I'm just bursting. I'm supposed to be on a diet as well, you know,' she giggled. She seemed very relaxed. I liked her more and more.

I said, 'That's one of the things I'd hate about being a girl: always having to go on diets, even if you've got an amazing figure like you.'

She blushed at the compliment (it was true as well). *What a shame*, I thought. *I'm going to have to send this evening crashing down now*.

I persuaded Leah to have a coffee. Then, for only the millionth time, I sneaked a glance at Nicole's table. She and her boyfriend were getting ready to leave. Excellent! Now I could totally concentrate on the grisly task ahead of me.

I figured, just before the coffee arrived was the time to slip Leah the not-so-great news (well, better than any of the other times). I said quickly, 'The thing is, owing to pressure of other commitments, Danny won't be able to see you very much in the future . . . but it's nothing personal. Honestly. It's just he leads such a fantastically busy life . . . in fact, he's the busiest person I know. I hardly ever see him . . .'

I stopped, because Leah was staring at me with such a

shocked look on her face. Then she whispered, 'He doesn't want to meet me again, does he?'

'Oh no, it's nothing like that.'

A look of wild hope appeared in her eyes.

'But he just can't give you the time you deserve.'

Leah said quietly, 'I do think Danny could have told me himself. I know he and I were just meeting as friends . . . but I still feel exactly as if I've been dumped.'

She got up, tears swimming in her eyes, and fled to the Ladies.

I'd so wanted to do this in a civilized, painless way. But it seems however jolly the build-up – and however much pizza is eaten – the end result is . . . Leah sobbing her heart out in the Ladies.

I squirmed about in my chair. I felt very guilty and I wasn't even the one not seeing Leah any more. I was so busy reflecting on all this, I actually forgot about Nicole for a few moments.

When I next glanced round her boyfriend was paying for his meal and saying something to the girl at the cash till which made her laugh. He looked a right poseur to me.

I idly wondered where Nicole had gone. And the next moment I saw her coming out of the Ladies with her arm around Leah. My stomach twisted with horror. It was one of those moments, which have a dream-like unreality. And before I could take in what was happening, they were both there in front of me.

Leah was saying, 'Sorry for running off like that but what you told me was such a shock . . . and this girl in the Ladies has been so lovely . . . Sorry, I don't even know your name.'

'Nicole,' she replied. 'And actually, this is so weird,' she continued, looking straight at me, 'but we know each other.'

Leah let out a surprised 'Oh,' and after Nicole said, 'Hello, Danny,' another considerably more surprised, 'Oh.'

'Well, hi there, Nicole,' I replied in this ghastly fake, cheerful tone. 'So how goes it these days?' I desperately wanted to move the conversation on, but Leah clearly felt she should correct Nicole's 'mistake'.

And she said to Nicole very politely, 'I can see how you got confused, because his best mate is Danny . . . But this is, in fact, Gary.'

Leah glanced at me for a quick nod of confirmation. Instead, I closed my eyes for a second. I just had a vague hope this might be one of those dreams you wake up from with a huge sigh of relief. I opened my eyes again. Unfortunately, everyone was still there. Nicole now had an extremely puzzled look on her face and I didn't blame her at all. It must be hugely confusing to go out with a boy you knew as Danny, only to be told a few weeks later that he is now called Gary.

Meanwhile Leah's eyes might have narrowed a little bit but she was still supremely confident about me being Gary. She went on waiting for me to say something, and finally asked with a nervous laugh, 'Gary is your name, isn't it?'

'Names, what do they matter?' I cried. 'We can get too hung up with labelling people, can't we?'

Neither Nicole nor Leah responded; they were both, however, looking at me rather oddly. 'But just to confirm the boring details,' I said as breezily as I could, 'yes, I am usually called Danny.'

Leah's eyes and mouth opened wide in blank amazement.

'But occasionally, to try and freshen things up, I give myself a different name –' here my voice fell away to a squeak – 'such as, for instance, Gary.'

Leah shook her head. 'I don't know what's going on here and you know what? I don't care either.' Then she gave me such a wounded look before rushing away.

I made to go after her but she called back, 'And please don't come after me, Danny or Gary or whatever your real name is.'

I sank back down in my seat.

Then Nicole said, 'Sorry for barging in like that . . . Have I messed everything up?'

'Oh no,' I said faintly. 'I managed that all by myself.'

Nicole went on. 'When I saw that girl in the Ladies I had no idea she was with you, she just seemed so upset . . . By the way, are you the Danny she was talking about? I'm still a bit confused about that.'

I couldn't reply. I couldn't even look at her, to tell the truth. I just wanted to crawl into the ground. And luckily I was saved further torture by her deluxe boyfriend striding towards us, looking so suntanned and happy. That was my excuse to cry. 'Really great to see you again,' and, after flinging down the money for the pizzas, scarper away as fast as I could.

When I told Gary what had happened he laughed and laughed – said it served me right for interfering. Later he called me to say he'd sent Leah an email (which was what he had wanted to do in the first place) saying why he had to finish meeting her – and also apologizing for my behaviour.

So there we go. Surely no one ever met their ex under

more excruciating circumstances than I did that night. Now Nicole thinks I'm some sort of madman who goes around giving false names to girls. As for Leah – well, any hope of ever seeing her, let alone going out with her, is completely lost now.

Not bad for an evening's work, is it?

Just one small consolation in all this. I know for certain James was lying. Nicole and her boyfriend couldn't have looked more friendly and happy.

I've resigned from dating girls now. I just haven't got the personality for it. Maybe when I'm twenty I'll go back to it – although I have mighty doubts even then.

To be honest, I'm enjoying my karate classes more.

And I really couldn't care what Nicole does any more. I'm well out of it.

Email to Leah

Hi Leah,

Just to confirm – yes, I am the real Danny. And I was the one who was supposed to meet you – but owing to circumstances beyond my control (my ex-girlfriend calling me seconds before our date), I was not in a fit state to talk to you and allowed my best mate, Gary, to substitute for me.

This was a huge mistake. I apologize unreservedly for that and for the past couple of weeks and the total mix-up today.

Maybe one day we'll meet up and smile about all this. And maybe we won't. Maybe you'd rather never see me again. I would totally understand that decision; it's all I deserve.

With my very best wishes for the future.

Danny

BELLA

Chapter 15

WEDNESDAY 26 AUGUST
4.30 p.m.

It's my own fault. I was too confident, too big-headed. So now it's happened – and it's far, far worse than I'd feared.

I was doing so well too. After I passed Phase One, I went on making 'spectacular progress' (Rupert's words – not mine). Yes, Luc was still floating round the edges of my mind, and quite suddenly I'd think about him and get a flashback.

But flashbacks are 'treacherous things' (another Rupert quote) and not to be trusted. Knowing that really helps me when they strike. And that pang of regret passes so quickly now. It helps a lot that I have things to distract me too, like my next Pilates class – or a chat with Rupert.

He's so charismatic – and intriguing. Especially the way he has a rule for just about everything. He's like a walking manual. But I like that as well, because when Rupert's about everything seems so simple. It's as if all the confusing messiness of my life is tidied away, and I feel sorted and calm and very strong. Well, I did until yesterday – that's when Andrea called.

She acted as if we were still the best of friends. 'Do you realize,' she cried, 'this holiday is nearly over and we're back at that concentration camp in just a few days?' She went on like this for a bit and I sort of joined in. Then she suggested we meet up before the new term starts.

So I went round to her house this afternoon. I knew there was no way Andrea and I could go back to being best friends again. So why was I seeing her? I suppose I wanted to show her how I'd moved on and was over her and Luc now.

Well, Andrea gave me a really big hug when I arrived, then started talking to me in this awful, treacly voice. She really thought this was going to be our big reconciliation scene. I almost felt sorry for her. How could she be so deluded?

It was very strange being in her bedroom again. My last visit, armed with scissors, still hung about in the air. I'm sure Andrea must have sensed it as well. She was certainly strange: fluttering about the whole time like a hen with an egg. She kept talking, too, about private stuff that only she and I would know about. I guess she was hoping these memories would bind us together again. But when Andrea stole Luc from me she didn't only change the present and future, but the past as well. And those old stories she was telling about us just didn't seem to belong to me any more.

Then she asked suddenly, 'So who's the boy you've been seen with?'

I started with surprise. 'What!'

'There are tons of rumours about you and him: he looks

about eighteen and is quite good-looking. Wears a suit. Come on, tell me absolutely everything.'

'Well, he's called Rupert,' I said.

'Oh yes,' she cried.

'And he's just one of the new friends I've made this summer, like Juliette and Kathleen and Zoe . . .' I reeled off all these names. I could tell Andrea was genuinely intrigued – and impressed.

'But how did you meet him, then?'

'Oh, after I started doing Pilates I met some people,' I said vaguely, 'and then I met some of their friends.'

'And now you've got an eighteen-year-old boyfriend?'

'As if,' I cried.

Andrea laughed but then said, 'You've changed, you know. Maybe it's your new hairstyle: you just seem so much older.'

And for a moment, disappointment looked out through her eyes, as if I'd let her down somehow by not staying the same. I really think she misses the old me who got overwhelmed with shyness whenever she met a new person, and admired Andrea for being so brash and dynamic. She wants the girl who was once cruelly nicknamed 'Andrea's shadow' back.

Shortly afterwards Andrea charged downstairs to get us some drinks. I sensed she was finding our reunion much more of a strain than she was letting on.

I got up and walked about. I had a bit of a headache, the kind you have after you've been stuck inside doing an exam all morning. Had I really only been here half an hour? Despite all our strenuous laughing, this had been a huge ordeal. *I'll gulp down my drink and go*, I decided.

Then, while prowling around Andrea's bedroom, I spied a photograph on her bedside table. Only it had been turned over. *Andrea has specially done that today to be tactful as it's of the one person we've so studiously avoided mentioning*, I thought. *And it's for the best if I look somewhere else. What's the point in seeing her special snap of Luc?* But then I thought, *No, I'm strong enough . . . I can do this.* I really believed I could.

So I turned the photograph over. It was a picture of Luc lying on a beach. He was grinning wickedly at the person taking the photo, while also looking at her with such affection.

Once Luc looked at me in exactly that same way.

Suddenly I flung the photo on to the floor as this great burst of rage took me over. It faded as suddenly as a crack of thunder. But it left me feeling choked with hurt and despair.

And it was as if I were experiencing all this pain for the very first time. It felt that raw and strong.

Sunshine came streaming through the windows, yet somehow I felt cold and clammy. I sat on the edge of Andrea's bed, with my arms wrapped around me.

'Sorry about the delay.' Andrea came dancing back into the room, a smile plastered across her face. My throat felt horribly dry even after I'd gulped my drink down, but I still managed to – as Rupert puts it – 'keep up a good front'. I even managed to pick up that picture of Luc which I'd slammed across the room, and slip it back in its place without Andrea noticing.

I don't think Andrea would have guessed, either, that

my head was now ablaze with pictures as memories of my time with Luc came flickering back to life once more.

More hugs when I left. 'We're going to stay in touch now,' cried Andrea eagerly, almost desperately.

'We certainly are,' I replied, my fingers firmly crossed.

'And one day you and Rupert must come out with me and Luc.' The very first time his name had been mentioned all afternoon. Andrea was looking right at me.

'That would be lovely,' I said.

Andrea rushed on. 'And I'm just dying to meet Rupert.'

I'll never introduce you to him, I thought. *He's nothing to do with you and never will be.* And I surprised myself with how strongly I felt about this. But I just said, 'Oh yes, you must meet Rupert. You'll love him. Everyone does.'

She nodded excitedly. I was amazed at how easily I'd fooled her. Did she really think I could spend an evening with her and Luc holding hands and whispering to each other?

Fury swept through me once more. And that's when I realized: the big relapse had started.

Even though I'd been warned, it still came as a shock. Especially the way the tiniest thing had triggered it off. Just turning over a photograph was enough for all those feelings to sweep over me – obliterate me. No, no, that was a silly thing to write. As Rupert says, 'Don't let life happen to you – stay in control.' And I intended to do just that. Still, I knew I needed his help urgently.

So I called him right away. Only he wasn't there. I just got his answer phone. I suppose I could have tried Juliette but right now it was Rupert I wanted. No one else. So I just left a message. I said, 'Rupert, it's Bella – and I think it's started. Call me as soon you can, please.'

5.00 p.m.

Rupert's going to be so angry when he finds out what I've just done. I've broken the very first commandment of Ex-Files. I've called my ex.

Yes, I rang Luc.

He answered right away. And I couldn't believe how easy it was to talk to him. He didn't sound at all apprehensive and wary as he had done last time, either. No, he was positively friendly, asked me how I was, as if he really cared.

Although my insides felt as if they'd just been scooped up, I carried on talking to him in the falsely cheerful tones I'd assumed for Andrea. And I kept everything very light. Then I told him about my afternoon visit to Andrea (although I'm pretty certain he knew about that already) and said how good it was to catch up.

After which I mentioned how Andrea had said the three of us should get together . . . with Rupert.

'Who's Rupert?' he demanded. Did his voice crack just a little bit now? Or was I imagining it? *No, he's jealous all right*, I thought, with a great surge of joy.

'Oh, Rupert's just a special friend,' I said airily, knowing that would inflame his jealousy all the more. I can be scheming when I have to be.

Then I continued, 'Before the four of us meet up I thought it might be good if you and me get together, just to clear the air . . . like Andrea and me have done today.'

Only a slight hesitation before he said, 'Yes, all right.'

'How about meeting up at Pizza Paradiso tomorrow?' I suggested.

A longer pause now. That was our special eating place – Luc's and mine. We had our first-ever date there. And our last.

'Or maybe you've gone off pizza?' I asked, with a little laugh in my voice.

'No, no,' he said, laughing faintly too. 'OK, Bella, we'll meet there tomorrow . . . How about seven o'clock?'

It was all arranged. I was beyond happy.

Then my mobile rang again. I was so afraid it might be Luc cancelling.

But it was Rupert.

He sounded anxious. 'How are you?'

'I'm great,' I cried.

'You left me a message . . .'

'I know,' I said. 'I'm so sorry but it was a false alarm.' Then I let out a huge sigh of relief.

Hated, hated, hated lying to Rupert! Felt as if I'd really let him down. But you see, when I saw that photo this afternoon the bottom just fell out of everything. Call it a relapse if you like. But I realized something too – that being with Luc really was the best time of my life. And that's not what Rupert would call 'a treacherous flashback'. It's quite simply the truth. I never felt so alive as I did during those months with Luc. And none of Rupert's rules can conjure that memory away. Now I've got a chance to see Luc again – and maybe get him back. And I can't let anyone – not even Rupert – stand in the way of that, can I?

PART FOUR

Fully Cured?

BELLA

Chapter 16

FRIDAY 28 AUGUST
9.45 p.m.

I received the shock of my life tonight.

I was waiting for Luc in Pizza Paradiso and seven o'clock had come and gone. He was late. Not a good sign. Was he going to ring up and cancel? Or how about if he turned up with Andrea on his arm?

No, Luc wouldn't do that to me. And I remembered he wasn't especially punctual when we went out together. I was usually waiting for him. I told myself to be more laid-back and stop watching the door. So I looked away for a good nine seconds. Then I spotted Rupert walking in.

I was stunned. What on earth was he doing here? That might seem a rather daft question, but somehow I only ever picture him sitting in the Copper Kettle. It was quite odd seeing him outside his normal environment. Still, why shouldn't he eat pizza? I wondered who he was meeting here: Juliette? Another girl? I even felt a tiny pang. Still, the main thing was he mustn't see me here with Luc. That would be totally disastrous. I held the menu up in front of my face. I kept it there for what seemed like centuries.

Surely Rupert must have sat down by now. I slowly lowered my menu . . . to see Rupert grinning at me. I was so horrified I forgot to breathe for a moment.

'Well, fancy seeing you here.' He sounded very jaunty.

'Yes, fancy,' I gasped. 'Are you, er . . . meeting someone here?'

'I certainly am . . . Looking forward to a great evening.'

'Oh good,' I said uncertainly. Then I watched Rupert sit down opposite me.

'Now, I hear you're something of a pizza connoisseur, so what would you recommend? Looking for something a bit adventurous . . .'

I could only gape at him. Finally, I asked in a small voice, 'What's going on, Rupert?'

'You mean, why isn't Luc here?' he said easily.

I lowered my head in deep embarrassment. I felt like a child who's just been discovered cheating.

'Well, he couldn't make it,' said Rupert, 'so I've come along as his understudy . . . Anyway, you were going to tell me which pizza to have.'

'Rupert,' I said, 'I still don't understand what you're doing here.'

His voice became very gentle. 'You've started having bad flashbacks, haven't you? The kind that just take you over. And meanwhile, hope is eating away at you like a worm in an apple. I sensed something was wrong the last time we spoke, so I set my investigators on to it, said it was urgent. They didn't let me down. Worked flat-out on this one and somehow they got wind of this get-together. By the way, I've called Luc and said you couldn't make it.'

I let out an angry gasp, more like a hiss. 'You had absolutely no right to do that.'

'I had every right,' he said calmly. 'I mean, what would you think of a doctor who let his patient roam the streets with a raging fever? You'd think he was a pretty poor doctor, wouldn't you?' He leaned forward. 'You're not your-self right now, Bella. You need protecting.'

'No, I don't,' I cried. 'I'd just arranged to meet Luc very informally to clear the air, that's all.'

Rupert didn't answer but he looked straight at me, taking in how dressed up I was and how much effort I'd made for tonight. Then he said, 'Enough of that, we've got an important decision . . . Which pizza are we having?'

'I can't eat anything now,' I cried.

'Why ever not? Am I such rotten company?' At this moment a waitress came over. Rupert beamed at her and ordered for both of us – for me he selected my favourite topping. How on earth did he know that?

'What did Luc say when you told him I couldn't make it?' I asked.

'Not much.'

'He must think it's so odd.'

'Not bothered about him right now,' said Rupert. 'You're the one in my care and I'm saying to you, no contact with him for at least a week.'

135

'And then?'

'Then the worst should be over . . . Relapses have usually burned themselves out after that.'

'You've got it all worked out, haven't you?' I said irritably.

'I know exactly what's happening to you,' he said. 'I recognize all the symptoms . . . That's why I had to take charge tonight.'

Part of me really liked the idea of him riding to my rescue when he thought I was in danger, but another part felt humiliated and insulted. He had no right to do what he did tonight.

'Before you called Luc,' I said, 'you should have got my permission. Just because I'm in the Ex-Files doesn't mean I'm one of your puppets.'

He sat back in his chair, and said quietly, 'I had to act fast to stop you making a catastrophic mistake.'

'It might not have been a catastrophic mistake,' I replied, equally quietly.

He didn't answer. Suddenly, he seemed subdued, even defeated. Well, good, he'd gone too far tonight. I sat there, unsmiling, hardly eating anything. Neither did he, even muttering at one point, 'Now I know why I haven't had a pizza for ages.' The atmosphere was the most strained it had ever been between us. He tried to make conversation. But he had to hack every word out of me.

He drove me home in silence, too. As we reached my house he said, 'You'll have some more flashbacks . . . don't trust them. And whatever you do, don't ring Luc –'

'For at least a week,' I interrupted. I was getting so weary of being told what to do all the time.

'And don't let your guard down for a second.' He said this the way a doctor might tell you to take some tablets twice daily. I felt a little glow of pleasure that I was being looked after.

But the glow faded very quickly. All I could think of was my missed chance with Luc. And I let out this loud, ugly sigh, just the way girls at school do when they think a teacher's being unfair.

I burst out, 'I can't tell you how upset I am by what you did tonight . . . I'll tell you something else. I think you're wrong about hope; it's not always bad. And without it, life's just so totally futile . . . which is exactly how mine feels now.'

Rupert turned and looked at me with such a pained, miserable expression on his face – and you really can't see a person look like that without your heart going out to him – that I was about to say something a bit softer when he broke out in a defeated whisper, 'Look, if you want to turn your life into a disaster movie, I can't stop you.'

'Thanks so much for your permission,' I cried. Then I slammed the car door shut and Rupert drove away so fast, one my neighbours came to the front door.

I know Rupert was highly disappointed in me tonight. And I hated him being disappointed. I want to please him so much. But he was in the wrong, not me. There's a big difference between looking out for someone and bossing them around as if they're three years old. And as for him calling Luc, I still can't believe Rupert did that. No wonder I feel cheated and very angry.

Chapter 17

FRIDAY 28 AUGUST
9.30 a.m.

I dreamed I was back with Luc. We were just walking through the town together. I don't know where we were going. Didn't really matter. And it was so easy and natural between us, as if the last five and a half weeks hadn't happened.

When I woke up, for a few crazy moments I even thought I really was with Luc again. It had felt that real.

Then came that awful thud of disappointment as I realized the truth.

There's no doubt about it, I'm having the big relapse. But does that mean my judgement is now shot to pieces? I honestly don't think it does. Also, I believe Luc really wanted to meet me last night.

Should I call him again to reschedule? No, it'd be much, much better if he rang me. So I'll wait until this evening. Don't want to appear too eager. And I've got a strong feeling Luc will be in touch soon.

7.00 p.m.

The evening took its first dramatic turn at around half past five.

That's when, out of nowhere, a massive thunderstorm came rushing up. Dad and I stood watching it, fascinated. We've always done that. I remember when I was about four or five gazing outside at the lightning streaking across the night sky with Dad's arm around me – and wanting the storm to go on and on. And, funnily enough, Mum, who was so bold and confident, absolutely hated storms. Dad loved to tease her. I nearly said something about that but Dad always goes very quiet when I speak about Mum now. So I didn't.

After the storm had finished, Dad carried on looking outside. He was waiting for Gloria. She was turning up in a taxi today. The second the taxi rolled up, Dad shot out with an umbrella. They splodged back into the house. Dad was driving them into London to see a play. (He had invited me as well, but I'd declined.)

Then the phone went for Dad and he was out of the room, leaving Gloria and me alone.

Gloria was sprawled out on the sofa, as fantastically self-confident as ever. I was sitting on the edge of a chair, with Tilly squirming about in my arms. You would think Gloria was the person who lived here and I was her guest.

'Well, how are you?' she asked. She was trying to act interested, pretending to be my mother. A shudder ran through me. I never, ever want her to be that. 'You're making more of an effort with yourself now, aren't you? Your hair certainly looks better these days.'

'Thank you,' I murmured. Silence fell. I was aware that Gloria's eyes were fixed on me as if she wanted to say something else. I shifted about uncomfortably. What was she going to say?

Then, to my surprise, she got up and stood over Tilly and me. She placed one of her beautifully manicured hands on top of mine. 'It's not easy, but you'll make it, you know,' she whispered. Dad had stopped talking about Luc weeks ago. He thought it was all over. But somehow, Gloria, of all people, had sensed I was still struggling.

Then Dad was back and there was more fussing about with umbrellas as he escorted her outside, and she settled herself in the car like some old-time movie star. But for one brief moment there she'd seemed almost human. I was very shocked.

A few minutes after Dad and Gloria had left the doorbell rang. I thought, *Dad's probably forgotten something.* I even wondered if it might be Rupert but I never expected . . .

They were both on my doorstep – Andrea and Luc. I reeled back in surprise. Andrea smiled at me. I think she was quite enjoying the impact of her visit.

'Have we called at a bad moment?' Drops of rain dripped off her nose but she still looked extremely attractive, I regret to say. Beside her, holding a soaking wet umbrella was Luc, looking at me with that open, soulful gaze which had so captivated me when I first met him.

'No, you haven't called at a bad moment at all. In fact, Dad's just gone out with Gloria (Andrea knew all about her and we even exchanged a little look). Do you want to come in?'

It seemed they did. We all trooped into the kitchen while Tilly tore around them excitedly. 'Someone's glad to see us,' said Andrea. Actually, it was Luc that Tilly was mainly pleased to see – he was a great favourite of hers as he usually played with her. I made coffee and hot chocolate for Luc (he always liked this best). Andrea marched around the kitchen, while Luc leaned against the door. Once I caught his eye; he smiled conspiratorially.

'It was so great meeting up with you on Wednesday,' Andrea said.

'Yes, it was,' I replied, lying to my back teeth. I kept sneaking more glances at Luc and getting little tingles of excitement every time. He was here in my house again. All right, he was being chaperoned by Andrea but still he was back where he belonged . . . with me.

'We called by,' went on Andrea, 'because we were worried about you.'

'About me?'

'Yeah, well you were supposed to meet up with Luc last night, weren't you?' I gave a little start that she knew about that and wondered who else he'd told. 'Only then Luc got a phone call, didn't you?'

She looked at Luc as if to say this is your cue to carry on the story. And he said very softly. 'A boy rang me, called Rupert. He said you couldn't make it tonight and I wasn't to bother you either. He sounded dead stern and fierce, like he was your dad or something.' He smiled suddenly – one of his puppyish grins.

'Obviously a very possessive boyfriend,' cut in Andrea, with a knowing smile.

But I hardly saw her. I was too busy noticing Luc; his smile had vanished and now he was looking genuinely concerned. I said, 'I'm afraid Rupert can be a bit over-possessive – especially when I'm having a meal with an ex-boyfriend.'

'I told you it was something like that,' said Andrea.

'He just seemed very controlling,' said Luc, 'and I didn't like that.'

'I'm sure Bella can handle him, can't you?' said Andrea.

'Oh yes,' I agreed.

'Are you seeing him tonight?' she asked.

'No, not tonight – probably tomorrow.'

Andrea nodded. 'Well, I'm afraid I've got to go – a boring tea with my uncle and aunt from Canada but they're only here for a few more days and if I'm late I'll never hear the end of it.' Then she added unexpectedly, 'But you don't need to rush away, Luc . . . You stay and chat with Bella – if that's all right with you?' She flashed me a questioning look.

'Yes, of course,' I said slowly. What was Andrea up to now? Was she being nice, giving Luc and me a chance to chat undisturbed? Or was this a little demonstration of her complete power? She was so confident she could leave Luc with me without a moment's concern.

It was all rather odd, but exciting as well. For here was my chance to be reconciled with Luc, handed to me on a plate by Andrea, of all people.

After she'd gone, Luc and I looked at each other very cautiously. We might have been two strangers meeting for the very first time. But I was all knotted up inside and I sensed Luc was too. Did he know Andrea was going to leave us alone?

He bent down and patted Tilly. And then he looked up and smiled at me again. He's got one of those smiles which warm you instantly, and makes him look so cheeky and attractive. People talk about charm: well, that's something Luc has in spades. He can pull you towards him with a look or a glance. And, unlike so many other boys, he never seems to put on an act. He'll just glide shyly into view – no posturing at all – and somehow you can't tear your eyes off from him.

I swallowed nervously, and then said, 'It's so strange seeing you again.'

'I've missed . . .' I think he was going to say, 'you' but was too embarrassed and instead just waved his hands around the kitchen.

'You've missed my kitchen,' I smiled teasingly.

He grinned. 'Yes, that's it. I haven't missed you at all, just your kitchen.'

'Well, I'm sure Dad will let you drop in and visit it any time you want.'

It was a silly, self-mocking conversation, just as we'd had so many times before. But right now it seemed the most precious thing in the world.

'Still, you've settled into a different kitchen now, haven't you?' I said lightly.

He lowered his voice. 'Feel bad . . . very bad about how it ended.'

'Snap.'

'You couldn't feel worse than me,' he said.

'I bet I could,' I replied hotly.

'I nearly rang you so many times.'

'Did you?' I asked sceptically.

'But I was just so frightened of making it worse.'

'It couldn't have been much worse.'

He reached forward and squeezed my hand. It was one of his little gestures, especially when we were out and we didn't want to parade our feelings like some couples do. So it was just a tiny, private show of affection that only we shared. And right then it knocked all the breath out of me. In fact, I had to look away.

Then he murmured, 'Andrea really misses you, you know,' and the mood between us was instantly smashed. I took my hand away from his.

'Do you want another hot chocolate?' I walked over to the sink.

He shook his head and went on, 'No, she really does. She told me once you are her only true friend.'

I gave a brief, highly ironic laugh and said quietly but firmly, 'She betrayed me.'

'Yes, all right,' he said quickly. 'But don't just blame Andrea. It isn't all her fault. In fact, she's the one who wanted to tell you weeks before . . .' He stopped, covered in confusion now.

I could feel my breath coming in tiny gasps. Then words floated up from somewhere inside me. 'I'm so sorry,' I hissed. 'I thought you and Andrea discovered love with a capital L when I was away on holiday. I had no idea this passion between you had been smouldering away before then.'

'Bella,' he cried sharply.

'No, please, I really want to know. How long had you and Andrea been pining for each other? Stop me when I get it right. One month?' I waited. He didn't answer. 'No, what about two months, or three months or how about the entire time you and I were going out together?'

He shook his head. He suddenly looked completely lost. Normally I'd have stopped there. There was something about Luc which made you want to protect him, but not now. My voice rose shrilly. 'No, I'd really like to know how long you and my best friend had been plotting this . . .'

He turned away. 'I should go.'

'No, don't go.' The words were tearing out of me now. 'I want to know what was wrong with me. Why did you dump me? Come on, tell me,' I shrieked.

Suddenly Luc whirled round and cried in a kind of screaming whisper, 'You just wanted so much from me. And you never left me alone. You took over my entire life . . . I couldn't breathe. I had to finish with you even if . . . even if I'd never set eyes on Andrea.'

He was actually shaking now. I shrunk back. Then, in a kind of trance, I said slowly, 'I didn't know. Why didn't you say something?'

'I tried to,' he hissed, 'but you never seemed to be listening.'

I sank down in a chair. I felt as if I'd just been hit very hard. I'd never for a moment suspected that Luc had been unhappy with me for so long. This was so terrible I couldn't react at all. It was as if I'd completely seized up.

He came over to me, slowly, with his head lowered. 'I shouldn't have said . . .'

'Yes, you should,' I gasped.

'I didn't mean to upset you,' he cried. 'That was the last thing . . . Andrea thought . . .' He faltered.

I looked up. 'Let me help you. Andrea thought leaving us alone would be a good chance for you to talk her up. Am I right?'

'She just wanted,' cried Luc, 'us all to be friends again.'

'Well, that won't be happening. Ever.' My voice sounded as sharp as steel. It even shocked me. 'Perhaps you'd tell her that. And would you do me another little favour?'

'Yes,' he said quietly.

'Don't ever call round to see me again.' My voice began to tremble. 'Not you . . . or her. Do you understand?'

He looked right at me. 'I understand exactly.' Then he announced, 'I suppose I'd better go.'

146

'Yes,' I agreed. 'Goodbye then,' I added crisply.

Without another word he walked out of the door and into the dim, wet night.

After he'd gone I just stood there like a zombie, still frozen with shock and horror. Outside, I could hear the rain rattling against the glass. It was such a restless night that I suddenly pictured myself running out into it, shrieking with misery and then . . . collapsing. Later, someone (my dad – but not with Gloria, please) would find me and carry me inside. Only my heart had weakened so badly I only had a few hours left to live.

I especially enjoyed my deathbed scene, as Luc rushed over to me, his face contorted with grief. 'Now that it's too late, I can see what I'm losing,' he cried. You're the finest person I know.'

I nodded my agreement and, with a forgiving smile fluttering across my lips, slipped away forever.

It was an incredibly silly daydream, but oddly comforting. Of course, it would never happen. For a start I'd never deliberately get wet, even if my heart was breaking. Also, I doubted if Luc would turn up at my deathbed in person (I'd be lucky to get a farewell email) and even if he did, and started blubbing, it wouldn't be because of his reawakened love for me. No, it would just be guilt for the girlfriend he'd wanted to dump for weeks and weeks and weeks because his heart had started its traitorous journey away from me, long before I ever went on holiday.

I started to cry then. Well, who wouldn't after hearing news like that? Great, tearing sobs that seemed to erupt out of me. Tilly sat whimpering beside me. I think my loud crying had frightened her, so I gave her a big hug and let her lick my face all over (unhygienic, but who cares). I didn't feel better exactly – but I was calmer now and just had this dull, heavy ache, like bad toothache.

I started thinking again about Rupert barging into my life last night. He knew seeing Luc would be a 'disaster', to quote the word he'd used. And he'd wanted to protect me from all that pain, wrap it away.

I felt such a rush of affection for him then. But when I called Rupert his answer phone was on so I left a message saying, 'It's me, Rupert, that awful, stroppy girl from last night. If you're still talking to me and haven't banned me from the Ex-Files –' I laughed nervously here – 'I need your advice urgently.

'You see, Luc and Andrea turned up here TOTALLY UNINVITED and I'd really like to talk to you about what happened. So when you have a spare moment, give me a ring. Take care. Bye.'

I'm sure Rupert will tell me off for letting Luc and Andrea in. But I don't care about any of that.

I just want to see him.

DANNY

Chapter 18

SATURDAY 29 AUGUST
Email to Danny

Hi Danny

Thanks for your email. Gary has also explained to me what happened and I think I understand it all now. I haven't told Juliette and Rupert about any of this, and I'd rather you didn't either.

One last thing: when I spoke to you on the phone (when you were pretending to be Gary, who was pretending to be you) I did notice how different you sounded. Not so much your voice (you disguised that pretty well), but you were gentler, more sympathetic. I thought, I'm talking to the real Danny now — well, I suppose I was, wasn't I?

Leah

Danny to Leah

Leah, thanks for getting back to me. I never thought you would. I was knocked out by your message. You took recent events amazingly well — sign of a quality person.

By the way, I know Gary took you bowling — but, interestingly, it's a favourite activity of mine too. So if ever you would like to go bowling with the real Danny — call me!

Incidentally, last night I passed my Phase One. Rupert and Juliette organized a little celebration for me. But they tell me I've still got a major relapse to look forward to (what fun!). So maybe you'd rather wait to go bowling with me when I'm completely cured. Or maybe you'd rather not go at all. The choice, of course, is entirely yours.

Best
Danny

Leah to Danny

Hi Danny

Yes, I'd love to go bowling with you.

School starts again (worse luck) on Tuesday. So how about meeting up on our last night of freedom, on Sunday night? Let me know if that's OK.

Best
Leah

PS Glad to hear you're planning to turn up in person this time, as I shan't accept any substitutes!!

Danny to Leah

Leah, I just had to say right away that Sunday night is highly OK to go bowling with you. I'll ring you shortly to firm up things.

My very best
Danny — the one true one

BELLA

Chapter 19

TUESDAY 1 SEPTEMBER

First day back at school. I'd been dreading it, but not for any of the usual reasons.

Andrea was practically the first person I saw. 'Hello,' she said in this affected but dismissive way.

'Hi,' I nodded.

The girl she was with – Lydia – totally ignored me. Then they linked arms and walked off together.

Andrea's clearly given up trying to make up with me. Luc must have told her what I'd said that evening they came round. But meeting her at school wasn't too bad, really – it was after school I hated. For there was Luc, in exactly the spot he used to wait for me – directly opposite the school gate, slouched against that large oak tree. Only he wasn't waiting for me any more.

I watched Andrea rush over to him and kiss him very fervently. Then she clung to his arm and they walked off dead slowly, as if they wanted to stretch out their every second together.

At one point Andrea looked around at me. A horrible, gloating stare as if to say, look what I've got. But I didn't let on that I'd seen her and even managed to keep a small smile on my face.

Inside, of course it hurt and hurt. Juliette had warned me that it would. She also said, 'The next time you see them together will be nearly as painful – but not quite. And each time it will go on hurting just a little less, until one day Luc and Andrea will seem a million miles away from you.'

Juliette has been so helpful these past few days but I do miss Rupert. I haven't spoken to him since that night at Pizza Paradiso. It's always Juliette I see now.

She told me, 'Rupert's had a lot resting on his shoulders lately, so he's having a bit of a break.'

Well, he certainly deserves one. But when I asked Juliette how long Rupert's holiday would last, she was very vague.

DANNY

Chapter 20

For the attention of Danny
THE BIG RELAPSE CHECKLIST

Have you displayed any of the following symptoms?

1. Started dreaming about your ex.
2. Begun remembering your time with your ex and are getting very nostalgic about it.
3. Had sudden overwhelming cravings to see your ex.
4. Keep being reminded of your ex (songs, etc.)
5. Think you've got a chance of getting back with your ex.

If you have ticked three of the following, stay on full alert: a big relapse could well be on its way.

If you have ticked four or more, your big relapse HAS DEFINITELY STARTED. There is no need to panic. But make sure you contact Rupert or Juliette IMMEDIATELY.

You have come so far – don't lose the final battle. Be vigilant at all times.

THERE'S NO ONE YOU CAN'T GET OVER.

WEDNESDAY 16 SEPTEMBER

I've come down with the dreaded relapse, haven't I?

Lately I've been feeling so far away from Nicole – and it's been great. But last night she oozed up from the deep and I had a dream about her. We were on a train going somewhere or other; we might even have been going on holiday because we were both in such a good mood. We were laughing and kissing in this carriage we had all to ourselves.

Then I woke up but I was highly alarmed because I know dreaming about your ex is a classic symptom of the big relapse. Other symptoms quickly followed, including tonight . . .

Tonight I had such a strong craving to see her that I ended up hanging around outside Colby's Bookshop. I was waiting to see her arrive for Teens Take Action, just as if she were some local movie star or something.

Some part of me knew what I was doing was dead stupid. But I didn't listen. I told myself I was only there to gaze at her – so where's the harm in that? And I could do nothing else. It was as if I'd been hypnotized. That's the only way I can describe it.

What saved me was that Ex-Files' checklist. I found it in my pocket (don't even remember putting it there, but there it was) and for a few glorious moments sanity surged through my veins once more. I called Rupert, briefly explaining my plight. He just said, 'I'll be right there.' No Spiderman hero could have acted more swiftly.

And before I knew it, a strong hand had fallen upon my shoulder. I looked up gratefully at Rupert. 'Hope you weren't having your tea or anything when I rang,' I said.

Rupert just patted me on the shoulder, as if to say when the big relapse strikes you down, food ceases to matter. He half-steered me away from the bookshop, cracking jokes as he did so.

After that Rupert and I went for a little walk. But already it was over. 'That was your first intense craving,' said Rupert. 'You'll almost certainly get some more. But next time it strikes, just keep saying to yourself, "I'm bigger and stronger than this."'

He went on, 'And watch out too for flashbacks. You'll probably get some very powerful ones. Only memories are tricky things – and right now not to be trusted. So be on your guard at all times.' Sometimes Rupert's like my coach. And tonight he certainly got me all fired up – and determined to beat this big relapse!

Just before I got home I had another craving – for chocolate. I was about to pop into my local shop when who should I see coming out of it but Nicole – with James. I quickly swerved away so they didn't notice me.

But I was amazed – first of all that Nicole wasn't at Teens Take Action. And secondly, why on earth were they frequenting my cramped, pokey, humble little shop? There are much better shops around where she lives. And she knows I only live up the road. Talk about inconsiderate. No wonder ice-cold rage shot through my veins.

I was in a bit of a state after that. So I went round to see Leah. She and I are really good mates now. In fact, I see her practically every night. I know all her family, too – I get on especially well with her mum. She thinks I'm a 'nice lad' – a bit of contrast to Nicole's parents, there.

Leah's very gentle but with this great sense of humour just bubbling under the surface all the time. And she's someone I can really talk to!

Anyway, Leah cheered me up tonight (we're very good at cheering each other up) and I feel really strong now.

Nicole might have come rushing back into my life today, like a river that's been dammed up. But this really was her farewell appearance.

And in about a week I should be in full remission from her, just in time for my birthday, in fact.

So on my birthday I should be rid of her forever.

Something to celebrate all right!

BELLA

Chapter 21

THURSDAY 17 SEPTEMBER

Every day after school Andrea's meeting with Luc becomes more dramatic. Often she'll squeal out his name from the school gates (sometimes Lydia will join in, making them sound like two cheerleaders). Then she'll pelt into his arms, acting as if he's just returned from a far-distant war rather than the school down the road.

And I know all this theatricality is at least partly for my benefit. Andrea's hurt that I've spurned all her attempts at reconciliation, so now she wants to really rub my nose in it, making me suffer just as much as she can.

More than once I've noticed Luc look highly embarrassed by Andrea's antics. I've even started to get waves of sympathy from some of the other girls, too. A few have even begun calling things while she's slobbering over Luc. But Andrea, who's usually so quick to notice which way the wind is blowing, seems blind to all this. She's so totally obsessed with making me feel bad.

This afternoon, though, something completely un-expected happened. Andrea was away so I assumed Luc wouldn't be hanging opposite the school gates. But no, there he was as usual. I guessed he hadn't realized Andrea was absent today. Well, I wasn't going to tell him. Let him wait for her all night. I didn't care.

But then Luc called, 'Hey, Bella,' and my heart took a sudden leap. It was as if I'd travelled back a couple of months to all those times he'd hung about for me.

He jumped in front of me, saying, 'Can I walk for a bit with you?'

'There's no law against it,' I replied gruffly. I told my heart to stop leaping about. Luc was an ex now. So I should be highly wary. In fact, the Ex-Files would say I shouldn't talk to him at all. I had all my wits about me, though. 'Andrea's away today,' I said.

'I know,' he replied. Then he added, in a low voice, 'I've been wanting to speak to you for days.'

'Oh, I'm here every afternoon,' I said lightly. 'No appointment necessary, just come up and chat away.'

'Bella.' The way he said my name, very softly, made me look at him. 'I said some things to you last time that I didn't mean. I've wanted to apologize ever since . . . and to say that we had some very good times together.'

'Well, I'm so glad you remembered them,' I said flippantly. 'That's made my year.' I turned away as if to say this conversation is now over. I had an awful lump in my throat, but I didn't want Luc to know it. That's why

I started walking faster. I spoke quickly too, in a voice just above a whisper. 'And it's all in the past now.'

He stopped and shook his head. 'You can't split your life up into neat little sections: that's my past, that's my present. It all flows together – Bella, it's all one.'

Luc often came up with philosophical nuggets like that. It was one of the things which made him stand apart from most other boys.

He went on, 'And us not speaking . . . I hate it. It really tears me up,' and his voice actually throbbed as he said this. 'I couldn't even tell you how much I like the way you've done your hair. It really suits you.'

The compliment caught me off balance. 'Oh thanks, I just felt like a change.' I could have added, 'And you know all about feeling like a change,' only my mood had totally altered. I even noticed for the first time what a lovely afternoon it was: earlier it had been raining, but everything was sparkling now and smelled so green. The perfect backdrop for Luc to say he wants to come back to me. This was what he was building up to, wasn't it? It had to be. I tried very hard to keep a hopeful look from breaking out all over my face. But my heart wouldn't be restrained: it was pounding loudly and shamelessly.

'I know I have no right to ask you anything at all,' he went on in this low, humble voice. 'Only I've missed you so much.'

'But you're with Andrea now,' I said gently, pushing this conversation forward.

He groaned. 'I know, and it's good,' his voice splintered

away, 'most of the time, anyhow. But I can't just extinguish all my feelings for you.' He stopped and gave me one of his soulful glances. Luc is such a master at that. But, funnily enough, this was the moment when the romantic music, which had been rising higher and higher, switched itself right off.

Instead, there was a sudden deathly silence and a horrible realization that Luc didn't actually want to go out with me again. No, he wanted more secret assignations like this, where he could gaze mournfully at me, confide all his troubles . . . and no doubt throw in a bit of snogging as well. Then, with lips quivering, we'd part until our next emotion-packed, top-secret encounter.

All at once it was as if a really harsh spotlight had dropped out of that beautiful, blue sky and was now beaming unmercifully on Luc. It made him look very pale and skinny (muscles were never part of his appeal) and so short.

It made me remember his laugh, too. Even then, it was the one thing I'd never liked about him. It was too nervous and high-pitched, like a kind of squeal a frightened puppy might make – and highly unsexy. How on earth had I stood it?

Suddenly I could see how very weak Luc is, too – and vain. And yes, sly. Yet, I'd placed my whole life around him. My only chance of happiness rested upon this boy because he had a lovely smile and smouldering eyes. Around that I'd created the perfect person. But actually, I'd been in love with someone who'd never really existed. And now he was falling apart before my eyes . . .

All the time I was thinking this, he was still whispering away and fixing his – even under my harsh spotlight – utterly bewitching eyes upon me. He really believed he was hooking me in once more . . .

Then we reached my house and he gave me his lost, little boy smile. And despite everything, I felt a definite tug of sadness. But it was the sadness you feel when you're looking at a film of a particularly good holiday. You miss it like mad for a few moments, but you also know it's over forever. You can never go back.

'Well,' said Luc, with a heavy sigh, 'I really want to see you again . . . but I don't feel I can hurt Andrea right now.'

He paused, confidently waiting for me to suggest another secret assignation, but I just said, 'It was so kind of you to walk me home, Luc – and I'm glad we've had this chance to say a proper goodbye.'

A look of complete shock crossed his face. His jaw even trembled a little bit.

'Take care of yourself, Luc,' I said softly.

'And you.' He managed one of his graceful smiles. But he still looked stunned.

And before, whenever he'd left my house he'd always turn at the end of my road and wave, but today he didn't look round once; he just carried on walking out of my life forever.

Later Juliette rang. I could feel her listening intently to what had happened today. 'The nerve of him,' she cried, 'wanting you to go from being his girlfriend to his bit on the side.'

162

'Well, he didn't put it exactly like that,' I said, feeling, for some reason, I had to defend him.

'But that's how it would have turned out,' said Juliette confidently. 'With the promise of him dumping what's-her-name dangled in front of you as a little teaser – but he'd never actually do it.'

Then I asked Juliette if this meant I was totally cured of Luc now.

'Oh no,' she said, 'it's not the end – but I think it's the beginning of the end.' She and I are getting on so well now. I really like her.

Yet, I still miss . . .

I asked her again tonight when Rupert's break would be over. She suddenly hesitated, then said she really wasn't sure.

FRIDAY 18 SEPTEMBER

I was doing some homework, when Dad brought me in a cup of tea. He was still in what he calls 'his slobbing-out clothes'. I said teasingly to him, 'Not dressed yet? Gloria will be here soon, and you know how she hates to be kept waiting.'

Dad gave an apologetic cough before announcing, 'Actually, I won't be seeing Gloria tonight.'

I looked up at once. 'Nothing wrong, is there?'

'Oh no, it's just we've agreed to . . . cool things off – it's all very civilized.' He made to leave.

'Hang on, Dad,' I said. 'You can't just deliver a newsflash like that and walk away. Was it you who decided to finish things?'

'Yes, I suppose it was,' mused Dad, as if he were remembering something which had happened years ago. 'Gloria wished to move things on, and I just didn't want a more serious relationship . . . It was all very civilized,' he said again.

Now, I'd never really hit it off with Gloria – at times, in fact, she reminded me very strongly of Cruella de Vil – but I couldn't help feeling a sudden flash of solidarity with her: a fellow dumpee.

I bet she had no idea Dad was going to finish it either. He's so deceptive like that: quiet, patient, long-suffering for ages, then suddenly, out of the blue, he'll make a big decision and nothing can sway him.

So I felt sorry for Gloria, but I can't pretend I wasn't also massively relieved. She was definitely not my idea of a stepmother!

I sensed Dad wasn't as calm about all this as he was pretending. I said, 'If ever you want to talk . . .' Then, using one of Rupert's phrases: 'I offer a twenty-four-hour listening service.'

Dad smiled slowly and said, 'Gloria was an admirable woman in so many ways.'

I did my best to agree with him.

'But,' he added, 'she just wasn't your mother.'

It was the first time Dad had mentioned Mum for absolutely ages. She was such a strong personality when she was alive: it always seemed odd that she could vanish so completely out of our lives. But I realized suddenly that wasn't actually true – and Dad was still trying to find her.

MONDAY 21 SEPTEMBER

The very first time I visited the Copper Kettle (feel as if I've been going there half my life now) I spotted a boy I vaguely recognized talking to Rupert. Later I remembered his name: Danny. He was a year younger than me and went to Luc's school.

The other day I saw him again. We smiled a bit uncertainly at each other but never spoke. Today, though, he came up to me. He's really quite good-looking, with dark, curly hair, a strong jaw and a perfectly shaped nose. He said, 'Excuse me, but you're in the Ex-Files, aren't you?'

'Yes, I am.'

He lowered his voice. 'So am I.'

I'd guessed that already, of course. Even so, he didn't seem a typical Ex-Files recruit, far too laddish and confident. But then, being dumped can happen to anyone. There isn't one particular type. 'So how are you getting on?' I asked.

'Passed my first stage all right. I bet you have too.'

'Yes.'

'But I'm now in the very last stages of the big relapse . . . Have you had that yet?'

I nodded. 'It's terrible, isn't it?'

'I tell you, if it hadn't been for Rupert and Juliette I'd have done some shocking things. Did they make you sign a contract?'

I nodded again.

'Scared the wits out of me, that did.'

I grinned. 'Me too.'

'I kept checking it for any secret clauses saying you had to pay them £8,000 or something. I thought there's got to be a catch to this somewhere. They can't just want to help you . . .' He lowered his voice even further. 'Met any of their secret investigators?'

'Just one, a girl from my school. One day I'd really like to do that.'

'Me too,' he agreed fervently. 'But you have to be trained up to be an investigator, so Juliette told me. I think she and Rupert have got the toughest job, though, listening to people going on and on about their troubles. Only last night Rupert sat with me –'

'Oh,' I interrupted excitedly. 'Is Rupert back from holiday, then?'

Danny looked puzzled. 'I didn't know he'd been away. I've seen him just about every night lately.'

So Rupert has, in fact, only been taking a holiday from me.

I must have really upset him that night at Pizza Paradiso.

And there doesn't seem to be anything I can do about it.

DANNY

Chapter 22

THURSDAY 24 SEPTEMBER

I've just found out something incredible.

Rupert came round to my house tonight. He stood in the doorway in his long, black coat, piling on the charm with my mum. She thinks he's someone I met at Teens Take Action and is dead chuffed by my new circle of friends.

But then Rupert put a hand on my shoulder and hissed, in a low, urgent voice, 'Let's take a walk.'

So we went out into the dark, glowering, wettish night, where Juliette was waiting for us with a huge umbrella. The three of us set off crouched under the umbrella. 'Well, this is cosy,' I said. 'What's going on?'

'Got some news for you,' said Rupert. 'We've found out something – thanks to our investigators, the great unsung heroes and heroines of the Ex-Files.'

'We couldn't believe it at first,' cut in Juliette. 'That's why we made our investigators double- and treble-check it.'

'We knew we couldn't break the news to you until we'd

done all the proper checks,' said Rupert suddenly. They were a real double act, both talking in low, rather flat voices, yet just beneath the surface I could pick up their excitement too.

'Well, tell me,' I cried, 'before I die of suspense.'

We stopped walking. The night was very still. No one seemed to be about, but Rupert's voice was little above a whisper as he said, 'The person Nicole has been passing off as her boyfriend is nothing of the sort . . . In fact, he's her cousin. The Ex-Files is now convinced no real boyfriend actually exists. It was all a con.'

There was a silence then, which was as loud as a yell. Finally, I cried incredulously, 'You're kidding me. I mean, why would Nicole pretend she's got a new boyfriend?' The answer had already flashed in my head but I wanted someone else to say it.

'Juliette and myself have applied the Sherlock Holmes principle to this problem,' said Rupert. 'Namely, when all other possibilities have been examined the remaining possibility, however improbable, must be true; in this case she did it to try and get you back.'

A couple of breaths tore out of me before I declared, 'Well, I never expected this . . . I really had given up all hope.'

'I know, you were making brilliant progress,' said Rupert proudly.

I asked, 'But why go to all the trouble of getting someone to pose as her boyfriend? Why not just come round and say she can resist my manly charms no longer?' I grinned sheepishly.

'She's just too proud,' replied Juliette.

'Or too scared,' suggested Rupert. 'After all, you might have slammed the door in her face. So instead, she cooks up a scheme that'll send you rushing round to her . . . and when that doesn't make you jealous –'

'She sends James round,' I interrupted, 'with that mad story of him hating her new boyfriend and offering to reunite Nicole and me. I bet that was a tough thing for James to do.' And as I said this I suddenly remembered him that Saturday morning standing in my kitchen, sweating with embarrassment. 'Nicole must have been very persuasive . . . or maybe he just felt very guilty,' I added. 'And when I saw Nicole in my road . . .'

'Oh, she's been there a few times,' said Juliette. Her voice rose mock dramatically, 'just hoping to accidentally on purpose bump into her dream boy.'

'I had my own stalker,' I cried, 'and never knew it.' I laughed. We all did.

But then, as we started walking again, Juliette said, 'Of course, if you'd gone along with James's plan, you'd have been reunited with Nicole weeks ago.'

'I bet you wish we hadn't interfered now.' Rupert said this very lightly, but I sensed both he and Juliette were listening intently to my answer.

I said slowly, 'I'd have felt a bit of a patsy if I'd fallen for what James had set up. So I think it's quite cool I didn't do that. Anyway, these past few weeks I've found out such a lot about myself and got to know Leah a lot better, not to mention you two. No, I'm really not sorry.'

Neither Rupert nor Juliette said anything but I knew they were pleased. I didn't say it to make them feel good, though. It is the truth.

And then it hit me. Nicole wanted me back! And I felt every happy emotion there was. I yelled out, 'Nicole wants me back!' I was ecstatic and just wanted to let it out. Then I said to Rupert and Juliette, 'So come on, what do I do now?'

And those two, who are usually so clear and definite about absolutely everything, actually looked at each other before replying. 'This is uncharted territory for us,' admitted Rupert. 'We've never had a couple get back together before.'

'So I'm making Ex-Files history,' I cried. I was just so high now.

'But earlier today,' said Juliette, 'Nicole was seen buying a birthday card by one of our investigators. We strongly suspect that card is for your birthday on Saturday. If we're right, then the card will be a good opportunity to go and see Nicole . . .'

'If that's what you want,' said Rupert.

'It really is,' I cried.

'Well, it looks like we might be redundant after tomorrow,' said Rupert, with mock gravity.

t my house he gave me one last piece of advice, emember, take it nice and easy with Nicole d don't come on too strong.'

e gave my hand a little squeeze. 'I'm really
170 ' she said.

e I couldn't just slip back into my house,

so I went for another walk. In my head I started picturing our reunion tomorrow, then our first date . . . and our second and third (that was an especially good one). It just went on and on. I tell you, daydreaming can be so exhausting.

Then I stopped off at Leah's. She picked up my mood of excitement right away. I told her everything. To my surprise she said, 'But isn't that a bit sneaky, getting you back with a trick?'

'Rupert explained that. He said she was scared I'd just slam the door in her face.'

'Oh, I see. Well, then, I'm very pleased for you.' She added, 'Just in case I don't see you tomorrow I'll give you your birthday card now – I've got you a tiny, weeny present, too.'

'You shouldn't have done that,' I said.

'Wait until you see it first, it's . . . Do you remember telling me how you found that frog in your garden and how much you like them? Well, now you need never be without one.' And she handed me a tiny little beanbag in the shape of a frog. It was made of cloth and was quite heavy and the frog's eyes wiggled when you shook it.

'I really, really like it,' I said. And I did. 'I'll make sure I never travel anywhere without it. It'll bring me luck, too . . . and it's just a top present. Thank you very much.'

When I said goodbye to Leah I felt suddenly choked. That's why I said loudly, 'You've been a really great friend . . . and this isn't the end of us. It won't alter us at all. We'll still go bowling and meet up . . .'

But really I knew it wouldn't ever be quite the same. I

think Leah realized this too, because she gave me a little hug at the door.

'I know you'll have the best birthday ever,' she called after me.

I believe I will, too.

So here's to Nicole and Danny, the sequel.

Chapter 23

SATURDAY 26 SEPTEMBER

I got Nicole's birthday card this morning, as the Ex-Files predicted. A very stylish card, too. It was the words inside that meant the most, though. Not the happy birthday bit, but what she'd written after that.

> *Danny, how are you? It'd be great to catch up sometime. I've just broken up with my boyfriend (it was mutual), so call round and see me, if you feel like it. Have a wonderful birthday. Love, Nicole X.*

The message couldn't have been much clearer, could it? I wanted to tear round and see her right away, only it was 7 a.m., which was a bit early. And anyway, my family had organized a special birthday breakfast for me.

The presents they gave me weren't bad, either – usually I just get a turnip or something ('Times are hard, blah, blah, blah') but today, they were halfway decent.

173

By the time breakfast was over it was after 9 a.m., late enough to call on Nicole now.

I practically ran all the way to her house and then hovered outside. I decided it was nerves, so I gave myself a little pep talk.

But still I hung about outside. It was so weird; I'd burned for this moment for so long. Now, here I was, just loitering about. I dug into my pocket and brought out that tiny little beanbag frog Leah had bought me yesterday. It was so cute I grinned to myself. And then, quite suddenly, I found myself moving briskly away from Nicole's house, and in quite a different direction.

Leah was just going into town with her family when I rolled up. But I think her mum sensed I had something important to say, because she said they'd wait in the car for her.

Leah was looking at me in a puzzled way as we went into the kitchen. 'Is everything all right?' she asked.

'No, not really,' I said. 'I got a birthday card from Nicole – well, look, here it is. Read it for yourself.'

She quickly read it, then looked up at me, smiling wanly. 'Well, she wants you back all right.'

'Yeah, looks like it. I've already been round her house.'

'Oh . . . so what happened?'

'Nothing. I didn't go in.'

Leah's eyes grew wider.

'I meant to, but I came round here instead, because while I was standing outside Nicole's house I felt all confused. Then I looked at that frog you'd bought me and it just hit me like a thunderbolt; that although it was Nicole I'd been chasing and dreaming about all summer, it was you I wanted to ask out, and straight away I stopped feeling confused. Not that I'm saying you should go out with me, as I'm certainly not the world's greatest bet. And I'm only just over my big relapse but . . . well, that's all really. It's enough, isn't it?'

Leah, who had been watching me really intently, said slowly, 'So let me get this straight: you were going to ask Nicole out until you looked at that silly frog I bought you –'

'It's not silly,' I interrupted. 'It's marvellous.'

'And once you saw that, you wanted to go out with me instead?'

'Not exactly . . . I mean, I've wanted to go out with you at the back of my head for days and days . . . but that frog just brought it to the front of my head.'

She shook her head. A smile played across her face.

'Sounds mad, doesn't it?' I said.

'Totally,' she agreed. Then she asked softly, 'So what about Nicole?'

'I did really like her,' I admitted. 'But she dumped me and well, now . . . it's you I want, no one else. Look, I shouldn't have sprung this on you . . . perhaps I can call later.'

There was a moment of total stillness while Leah just stared at me, with her eyes very wide. And then her beautiful arms were holding me very tight.

The kitchen door suddenly flew open and her little brother whined, 'Oh, come on, Leah, hurry up.'

I took both her hands in mine and held them against my face. 'I'll be back,' I whispered.

'I'll be waiting,' she whispered back.

And then we both laughed and I walked outside with her hand in mine and then Leah's mum jumped out of the car, looking very happy and everything just seemed so funny and brilliant . . . well, everything except . . .

Nicole will have got my note by now. I felt I should at least answer her card right away and not leave her hanging about waiting to see what I was going to do, because that's just sheer torture, I should know. So I wrote this:

Dear Nicole,
Thanks for my birthday card – it was a great surprise.
Sorry to hear you have split up with your boyfriend.
I am now seeing Leah. Lots and lots of luck to you.
With kindest regards,
Danny

I wanted her to know that I'm with Leah – yet in a tactful way. Of course, it's mad really. All summer I've dreamed about getting back with Nicole. And now, when I finally get my chance . . . it's as if the spell is broken. She can't be more surprised than me.

I suppose the truth is that Nicole and I loved the buzz of our first meetings and after that we thought everything was going to be so shiny and brilliant.

Yet it was never quite real. I mean, there was a definite attraction and we did get on, but somehow we never really

176

fitted into each other's lives. And I always felt I had to keep proving myself to her. I could never just be myself. Maybe she felt that with me, too – and that's why she went through all that charade of a pretend boyfriend.

Meanwhile, all my feelings for Leah have just crept up on me . . . We were mates, good mates, and then today I realized there was no one else I wanted to be with, except her.

There are no hard feelings about Nicole, not on my side, anyhow. And what I put at the end of my note to her today – the part about wishing her 'lots and lots of luck' – I really meant that.

BELLA

Chapter 24

SATURDAY 26 SEPTEMBER

Red and blue balloons were hanging outside the Copper Kettle tonight. They were in honour of my graduation.

I'd sort of had a hint that something was in the air, especially as two nights earlier Juliette had come round and asked me all these questions about Luc (when was the last time I'd seen him, thought about him . . .).

But I still hadn't expected a massive banner inside the Copper Kettle saying, 'Well done, Bella'. Funny how snug and safe I felt in here. It was like a little nest. Just breathing in its warm scent of chocolate and scones now seemed to make me feel instantly at home. Who'd have thought it, the Copper Kettle turning into my second home? What a very bizarre summer this has been.

Zoe had come back for my graduation ceremony. And Juliette was there with Kathleen and Kathleen's mother.

But no sign of Rupert. He'd just vanished out of my life. And not even the sight of a massive chocolate cake could lift my spirits. But then there was a sharp knock on the door (the Copper Kettle was closed, of course) and there was Rupert, silhouetted in the doorway.

He looked at me quickly, smiled and then went over to Juliette. I told myself not to keep gazing at him – be calm, be casual. But I was so totally delighted to see him there.

It was Juliette who presented me with my graduation certificate though. She said, 'You've done so well, Bella, we wanted to put this event on for you. Congratulations on letting go of the past and being ready to move on again.'

Everyone clapped and Kathleen quipped, 'This is even more moving than the Oscars.'

Then I had to cut the chocolate cake. Anyone looking in through the window at that moment would have thought it was a private birthday party or that I'd just passed an exam or a driving test. Actually, I did feel as if I'd really achieved something. And later I gave Juliette £20 towards the Ex-Files' expenses. She didn't want to take it, said it was too much, but I insisted.

I said to her, 'I really hope this isn't the end of me and the Ex-Files. I'd love to become one of your investigators.'

'Now, we were hoping you'd say that,' she replied. 'We have a special training programme for our investigators but I'll tell you about that next week. Right now I have one last task to perform.' Then she produced the canvas bag, with my name on the front.

'The day you joined the Ex-Files,' she said, 'we asked

you to store away all your photos and mementos. We're inviting you to have another look at them and tell us what you'd like us to do with them. You can, of course, have them all back, if you wish. It's totally your decision. Take as long as you like,' she added, handing me a key.

I slowly opened up the bag, cautiously, as if I were expecting something to spring out at me. The contents inside had a forlorn, abandoned look, as if they knew they were in the waiting room for the scrap heap. I reached for a few photos and began skimming through them. I felt a tiny pang of sadness as I saw Luc and me looking so at ease together. I almost wanted to cry out a warning to the me in those pictures: 'Don't get too happy, it isn't going to last, you know.' But already, those pictures seemed to belong to another time as faraway as those shots of me starting at my nursery school. Really ancient history.

And nothing made any impression on me, except for the ring which Luc had given to me. I started remembering the moment Luc placed the ring on my finger. 'This is with all my love,' he'd whispered. 'All my love'; people use that phrase so easily, then suddenly they've gone, taking all their love with them and leaving you with absolutely nothing.

I flushed guiltily as if everyone could hear my bitter reflections. I certainly sensed they were all watching me keenly. 'Is this my last test?' I asked brightly. 'I tell you, this all feels so long ago now. And, Juliette, I'd like you to dispose of the entire contents of this bag.'

There were claps and gasps, too – one of which was

from me. I hadn't quite intended to go that far. So I added, 'But would you mind if I just keep this?' I picked up the ring.

Did a flicker of disappointment cross Juliette's face? I'm not sure. But she just said crisply, 'Feel free to keep whatever you want, Bella. The Ex-Files has only borrowed them for your own personal safety.'

'Well, I think you need another piece of chocolate cake after that,' said Kathleen. She introduced me to her mum, who knew all about the Ex-Files.

She said, 'You probably think the Ex-Files is a very modern idea but it's also a very old one, you know. When I was growing up you knew all your neighbours. Now we're all scared to even look at each other. Who wants to live like that? We all need to feel part of something.'

Later Zoe came and spoke to me. And, finally, Rupert strolled over. 'I'm unbelievably proud of you,' he said quietly.

'Thanks,' I replied, feeling shy all of a sudden. I added, 'Thought you'd forgotten all about me.'

'Impossible,' he said in his loud, jokey way. But then his voice became much lower. 'That night at Pizza Paradiso, I went way beyond my remit.'

'No, you didn't,' I burst out. 'If I'd seen Luc it would have been a disaster. You were only stopping me from making a fool of myself. I see that now.'

'I got over-involved,' he said firmly. 'We have our own Ex-Files code of practice, you know. And I stopped being professional that night. That's why I took myself off your case – but Juliette's kept me fully informed. And I think she's done a fabulous job.'

'So have you,' I said firmly.

He looked at me. 'Just never forget . . . all endings are also beginnings – cheesy, but true. Life's all about looking forward, not back.'

'Is that your last piece of advice to me?' I asked with a little smile.

'My very last nugget of sheer gold.'

'And you're off to Birmingham University soon?'

'Tomorrow,' he said.

'Tomorrow!' I gasped. 'I had no idea it was as soon as that . . .'

He looked as if he was about to say something else but then Zoe came over and he went off with her, probably thinking what a lucky escape. Perhaps it often happens to him: a girl who he's helping suddenly transfers all her affection to him. Maybe he even tells Juliette, 'Would you believe it? Another girl's got a crush on me. That's three this month.'

And, of course, that's all it is – a stupid little crush. I was vulnerable and saw him practically every day . . . Only Rupert said he'd got over-involved in my case. Why was that? Was it because he was starting to care for me? Was it?

Wouldn't that be just like a boy – the moment he feels something, he can't come and tell me about it. Oh no. Instead, he runs away. Although, no doubt Rupert would wrap it up by saying he was being professional. But he cares for me, that's the important thing.

A few minutes later Rupert got a call on his mobile. He was 'on duty' tonight, which seemed a bit tough as he was leaving for university tomorrow, but I could sense his and Juliette's enthusiasm and excitement over a possible new case. And Juliette, for all her seeming calmness and laid-back air, really was as much a zealot for the Ex-Files as Rupert.

'You've got no time to go to university, Rupert,' said Kathleen. 'Got a full-time job here.'

'I know, but I'm leaving the Ex-Files in excellent hands,' said Rupert looking proudly at Juliette. 'And I'll be popping back from time to time.'

He said a collective 'Goodbye' to everyone. And suddenly I knew I couldn't let him leave like this. I had to speak to him one last time. So I rushed after him.

He was standing outside, looking up at the sky. There was a low, full moon making everything look oddly unreal, like a film set which could be wheeled away at any moment. Maybe this was what gave me the confidence to call out his name and then cry, 'I just wanted to say thanks again. And I'll miss you more than I can say, and perhaps we could meet up one night . . . even go back to Pizza Paradiso.' I smiled hopefully at him.

'Bella, if we started going out with the people we helped – well, it would just change the whole nature of the Ex-Files. It just can't be done, I'm afraid,' he said gently, and yes, a bit regretfully.

'But how about if someone still feels the same about you when you come back at Christmas, that'd be different, wouldn't it?' I cried eagerly.

He looked at me, smiled and started walking away.

'Wouldn't it?' I cried after him.

He suddenly turned round and his face broke into this brilliant smile. 'See you at Christmas then, Bella,' he yelled.

My heart soared for the rest of the evening. It was only when I was nearly home that I realized something: the ring that Luc had given to me – which I once said meant more to me than anything I owned – well, I'd only gone and left it behind in the café.

Kathleen will find it and keep it for me, I'm sure. It wasn't that what bothered me. It was the way I'd been so careless over something very precious.

I laughed out loud with shock.

It can't have been that precious any more, or I'd have remembered it. So here's more proof that I really have begun to let Luc go and am ready for the next chapter of my life.

And Rupert said he'd see me at Christmas.

I've been chanting those words over and over to myself like a charm. So he'll be in that next chapter for certain. And then . . . no, I mustn't speculate; no more daydreams.

I've got more Ex-Files work to do first. I'm going to learn how to be an investigator.

So I'll just whisper this once in the very last page of my diary: Rupert, I love you with my whole heart.